CHASING
AUGUSTUS

ALSO BY KIMBERLY NEWTON FUSCO

Beholding Bee

Tending to Grace

The Wonder of Charlie Anne

CHASING
AUGUSTUS

Kimberly Newton Fusco

ALFRED A. KNOPF
New York

THIS IS A BORZOI BOOK PUBLISHED BY ALFRED A. KNOPF

Visit us on the Web! randomhousekids.com

Educators and librarians, for a variety of teaching tools, visit us at RHTeachersLibrarians.com

Library of Congress Cataloging-in-Publication Data is available upon request.
ISBN 978-0-385-75401-9 (trade) — ISBN 978-0-385-75402-6 (lib. bdg.) —
ISBN 978-0-385-75403-3 (ebook)

The text of this book is set in 11.5-point Administer.

Printed in the United States of America
September 2017
10 9 8 7 6 5 4 3 2 1

First Edition

For my family, the best part of everything

PART 1

1

My grandpa Harry says vinegar runs through my veins and I am too impatient for my own good.

He says I stomp around like a moose half the time and I am proud, prickly, and rude.

Also, I am thin as an eel and, come to think of it, not much better to look at, either.

Hornets whirl up in me when my grandpa talks like this, I can tell you that. I read in my encyclopedia of facts—*The World Book of Unbelievable and Spectacular Things*—that if you wanted to cuss someone out in the Middle Ages, you called him a *clay-brained boar-pig*, so that's what I say to Harry.

"What?" he sputters. "Where in the name of Pete did you pick that up?"

I let my grandpa think about it as the afternoon train

rumbles into town and shakes our skinny apartment beside the tracks. Grit from the sandpits sifts like sugar through the window screens. Harry swallows the last of his sardines and crackers with a big gulp of black coffee, pushes the newspaper away, and grabs his fishing hat. "Don't you dare go anywhere on that old bike," he growls. "I don't care if school just let out for the summer. Thunder's rolling in."

When he stomps out, his gruff Marines voice marches right after him. He slams the door and the picture of me, my dog Augustus, and my papa flips on the floor. I pick it up, swipe off the grit. Of the three of us in that picture, I am the only one left.

I call Harry a *loggerheaded-maggot* and about a thousand other cusswords as he walks up Main Street to the donut shop, which he took over after my papa's stroke or else we would lose our shirts. I throw my report card in the trash and shove it to the bottom under all the coffee grounds. Then I rush into my room for my goggles and check the map of our town that I hung in the back of my closet, where Harry never goes. Each day I pick a new road to hunt for my dog, keeping track with a trail of stickpins.

Harry says you can't keep a big sloppy dog like Augustus in our skinny apartment, so it's best to forget him. A year is too long for a dog to remember a kid anyway—so put a lid on it.

My grandpa forgets how much you can love a dog or he would never say that. My dog slept on my bed and I fell asleep to his heart beating. He was the true-blue friend of my soul until that awful day my mum gave him away and flew back to California, where she is a lawyer now.

That's when I learned the real way of things: When you lose your dog, there's a hole in your heart as big as the sun. Your head aches all the time and you are so empty inside because you are half the girl you used to be.

For this reason, I swoop down our steep steps, past Eddie's Barbershop on the first floor (where there's always a bowl of M&M's waiting for me), and out onto Main Street, my goggles flapping and clapping behind me.

And I do not let the thunder inside Harry get in my way.

2

I call my bike the Blackbird.

It has one gear that works and rust spots the size of silver dollars and brakes that clamp only when they feel like it—but you don't really need to stop when you fly. You just need to land.

The Blackbird was my papa's bike when he was a boy, and the wire basket in the front is rusted through, the fenders are crunched, and the front wheel squeals and wobbles like an old washing machine off balance, but if you knew my papa, you'd keep fixing it, too. He had what is called a listening ear, and my bike does, too—you can tell the Blackbird anything when you ride and things start feeling better. Plus, it has a bell that sounds like an old goose honking, and folks tend to get out of your way.

I pull the Blackbird out of the toolshed behind our apartment building and lean it against the fence. Already the wind from the storm coming bends the thin maples on Main Street until they are looking at their feet. They could use a pep talk.

I hurry with the worst wheel first—the front—but Harry's old wrench won't grab hold because I've tightened the nut so many times I stripped the threads. Each time I try, the wrench slips.

My head pounds. The wind sends grit from the sandpits *pling-pling-pling*ing into my face. Our neighbor Mrs. Salvatore rushes out to the clothesline and pulls a bleached sheet off and tosses it in her wicker basket. I am careful to keep my eyes straight on what I am doing without any wavering at all because Mrs. Salvatore has a sixth sense about things. She can smell something fishy the way an old hound dog can smell mackerel in a can. Just one whiff of something out of place and she'll badger you until she gets to the bottom of things.

My headache roars. Grizzlies gnaw behind my eyes. I get the wrench to twist a quarter of a turn before it slips off.

"Rosalita!" Mrs. Salvatore yells, snapping sheets behind me.

I force the wrench, but I do it too hard and it slips

again. *God's bones*, I snort, which is another good cuss from the Middle Ages. My papa and I discovered this one when we read my *World Book* together, which has a full list. After that we made up our own—*cow-pocked rogue* (my papa's), *cockroach-breath* (mine).

There is a loud crash in Mrs. Salvatore's apartment and one of her foster girls screams at one of the boys for changing the channel, and since we live in such an old apartment building with rattling windows, thin walls, and hardly any insulation at all, you can hear everything—even when somebody pees.

Mrs. Salvatore yells, "You stop that, Francesca, you hear?" and when she catches me looking up, she snaps, "Night and day that girl is going to be the death of me. What did I ever do to the good God in heaven to deserve a girl like that?"

I don't know. I have no idea why she keeps all these foster kids when she already raised a bunch of her own.

My head throbs. My *World Book* recommends ice for headaches, so I rub my brow with the plastic baggie I filled with cubes from Harry's freezer.

Another train rumbles in, shaking the toolshed, the apartment building, and the ground beneath my feet. I pinch my lips in a straight line, squeeze the wrench, and turn, but not too hard this time. This is not easy when your heart is a rubber band snapping back and forth and you are in such an awful rush to find your dog.

I breathe in, twisting the wrench very slowly, and—bingo—the nut turns, the wheel tightens. I breathe out.

There is still a little wobble, but that is bound to happen with a bike so old. My papa had me when he already had gray hair, and the Blackbird is no spring chicken, either. This is why Harry says it belongs in a museum.

I pull on the swimming goggles I snuck into my pocket at the Church of Our Risen Lord thrift shop. I am riding out by the sandpits today, one of the last places on my map without a stickpin, and without the goggles I couldn't see through the whirling grit. I strap on my helmet and wheel my bike across the yard.

The clothesline pulley screeches like an oiled pig. "Rosalita Gillespie, I want you to come over and meet my new foster boy, Philippe."

When pigs fly.

I climb on my bike and test the gear lever, but it is stuck on third, the hardest to pedal, the one that forces me to stand when I ride uphill, and sometimes I even have to walk. I test the brakes, but the pads freeze before they clamp the wheel.

Mrs. Salvatore tells me how the new boy loves Monopoly, which I hate. *God's bones.* When she yells that my grandpa wouldn't want me going anywhere with this storm coming on, I shake my head and point to my helmet like I can't hear, but I can hear just fine and what I am really hearing is my dog's heart beating, I can tell you that.

3

I press my chest into the handlebars and shoot past the donut shop. The big coffee sign out front still blinks my papa's name—JACK'S DONUTS—on and off. Harry hasn't changed the sign.

I fly past St. Camillus Rehabilitation Hospital, where my papa's been since those first few terrible weeks. I do not allow my eyes to glance at his window or at the roses waving me in.

The wind picks up and the overhead wires hum. My chain clatters as I turn onto Maple Street, the road where I used to live. Someone is sitting on my old porch swing, watching the storm move in, and I picture my papa there, the smoke from his pipe swirling around his head, the smell of cherry tobacco scratching my nose.

I pedal faster. The Blackbird's front light rattles. The seat is cracked down the middle and pinches. My papa was going to help me fix it, but we never got around to it.

The milk truck roars behind me as I pedal up the first hill. The heat of the engine scorches my neck and the milkman swerves around me, yelling, "Storm's coming!"

I lower my head and push on. Already I am out of breath and I have a stitch in my side, but the spring under my seat bounces and squeaks and tells me not to be a quitter. It is good to have a bike that pushes you on. My tires skid in the gravel and at the top of the next hill I fly the Blackbird straight down, holding my feet out in case I need to stop.

The milkman hates dogs, and they hate him, but I never heard of any dog in the history of our town that hated him worse than my Augustus. He would chase the truck from one end of Maple Street to the other, and he'd growl and bite at the tires like they were cats. He'd put up such a ruckus I'd have to lock him in the house on milk days.

The milkman hogs all conversation at the donut shop by telling how he got chased by this dog or bit by that one or how a dog as big as an elephant jumped on him when he was carrying two gallons of milk into somebody's house. I am careful to keep track of every-thing.

Yesterday he told the folks sitting at the counter that he saw a big galumph of a dog out by the sandpits.

"Thought it was a bear."

I only ever saw one dog that looked like that.

4

Gravel crackles under my tires and the clanging clashing sounds from the sandpits fill my head.

Folks in other places say we are the grittiest town on God's sweet earth and who wants to live here? But what we really are is a town filled with folks who know how to press on and make do.

For this reason, we do not hang hammocks, we do not picnic when the wind blows, and some days, after a dozen sand trucks have driven down Main Street, we can surf the blacktop in our sneakers.

Other than our neighbor Mrs. Salvatore—who is a stubborn mule about that and every other thing—we do not hang our clothes on the line. We use Pine-Sol and Windex and keep track of wind direction the way some folks watch for snow.

In our town summer is hardest, and we know if we wash our kitchen tables in the morning and leave the windows open, we can come back at night and write our names in the grit on our tabletops. We do not pitch tents or barbecue, and we learn to love swimming when we are babies because there is no better way to get the dust off your back than a dunk in one of our old millponds.

My papa knew that eating a sweet donut after a long dusty day in a sandpit town like ours tends to perk you up. And, as he got everyone to believe, nothing gets the grit out of your throat better than a tall mug of his steaming black coffee.

I know other things—like how mums who don't like grit move to California when you are still a baby, how you don't need to bother with fancy shampoo because nothing scrubs the sand off your scalp better than Head & Shoulders, and, now most important, if you don't do something about all the grit in your life, things tend to jam up something awful.

5

The rain begins, first as a soft patter against my arms, then a steady *thrum thrum thrum*.

As it hits the road, puffs of grit burst in front of me. The quitting thoughts begin—the ones that tell me if I haven't found my dog by now, I'll never find him. I make myself think victory thoughts and pedal faster.

I lower my helmet. I have hunted for my dog almost every day for over a year and I keep going by imagining how it will feel to hold him in my arms, to bury my face in his warm clumpy dog fur, to snuggle so close I can feel his heart beating. In those old romantic movies Harry loves to watch, there is always a scene where the boy and the girl find each other after a very long time and they wrap themselves around one another, sometimes rolling down a hill and laughing, always with tears running over their cheeks. That's how it will be for me and my Augustus.

My papa was not too good about putting the Blackbird away when it snowed and rained, and now the old plastic handgrips pinch like sand crabs. I loosen my fingers and pedal slower because my tires are pushing through wet sand.

Thunder growls. A red Camaro roars up, horn blaring. It is Avery Taylor, one of the baggers at Shop Value, the star of the high school hockey team who everyone at the donut shop says has a college scholarship in his back pocket, but I wonder who would give money to somebody who tied the smallest boy in the whole second grade to a tree in front of the house where the terrible German shepherd Gorilla Dog lives?

I pedal faster as Avery Taylor swerves close, rolls his window down, and howls, "Get off the road!"

I push on. Rain streams inside my shirt and down my arms. Leaves whip into my sprockets and clack and snap. Two dump trucks lined up at the sandpits, their lights on, their windshield wipers whipping, wait for me to pass. As they pull out and the engines grind and the wheels slap against the wet road, a driver leans out and yells, "Go home!" and points to the sky.

I shake my head like I can't hear and shoot ahead,

listening for my dog's heart beating as the wind spits grit into my teeth.

In the next moment, the sky lights up and the first bang of thunder claps in front of me. The hairs on my arms split, the nerves in my neck twist. My dog wasn't afraid of anything but thunder.

The trees brace themselves, the ground waits. I try to remember what *The World Book of Unbelievable and Spectacular Things* says you are supposed to do in a storm like this, but the only page I can remember about lightning is the one with seven dead cows lying on their backs—their hooves raised stiffly in the air—and this hardly helps at all.

Rain falls so hard it snakes into my goggles, and I have to pull them off and toss them in my basket. My heart rushes, my blood pumps. Harry's going to thrash me.

A bolt of lightning wallops a tree and bark snaps and sparks pop. Smoke fills my nose. Finally, after hemming and hawing, I turn my bike around—this is too much, even when you would do anything to find your dog, even when your dog is terrified of thunder and you know, big bear that he is, he could be shaking under a tree somewhere, his big gooseberry eyes lonely, scared, and miserable.

I remember hearing a long time ago that if I ever got caught in a lightning storm, I should squat on the ground away from all trees and bury my head in my knees. I drag my bike off the road and hunker down, feeling like a wet onion.

I am interrupted when a black jeep with a duct-taped roof rumbles up over the hill.

The pounding rain makes my teeth chatter and pastes my T-shirt to my back, and the thunder banging all around me makes me jump—but these are not the reasons I shiver.

6

Most folks don't call her anything but Swanson.

She's not very old, not very young, but sort of in the middle, like my papa. She lives by herself on an old farm on the other side of town and never talks to anyone. My papa told me her mother died when she was a little girl and she never spoke after that.

Every winter thousands of crows roost in her pine trees, and television cameras and newspaper reporters line up, but since she doesn't talk, she runs into her little house, closes the curtains, and stays there until everyone gives up and goes home.

Keeping to yourself like that just makes the rumors swirl. Kids all over town say she shoots squirrels and can catch you no matter how fast you run and they dare each other to knock on her door, see who can steal apples from her tree, place wagers on who can make her talk.

Avery Taylor set up a betting pool when he was in sixth grade to see who was brave enough to break into her barn and climb her hayloft—at midnight.

The jeep rumbles to a stop. The engine trembles in the cold, the window rolls down. Swanson's red-checked hunting hat is pulled low and covers most of her bone face. I smell the warm wet wool.

I take a few steps back, trying to disappear into the rain. What's she doing out here? Her farm is on the other side of town, where apple and peach orchards grow.

My papa used to say her father was meaner than a skunk and she doesn't have anything and never did. He was in the same grade and she wore shoes so big they slipped off her heels when she walked. She kept to the shadows and made herself so invisible that it was weeks before anyone noticed she wasn't going to school anymore, and the only reason anyone figured it out was that the *flap-flap-flap* sound of her shoes was silent.

My papa used to give her free donuts. Harry says she's a piece of work.

I try and melt into the rain as Swanson rolls the window down further. All around me thunder booms, rain falls in sheets; another clap of lightning hits and Swanson points to the passenger door. No kid in her right mind would ever climb into that jeep. I shake my head, rush to my bike, get a running start, and jump on. My goggles and helmet bounce in the basket because I don't take time to put them on.

7

It is nearly suppertime when I race a soaked Blackbird into town and past the big house with the sweeping lawns on Main Street where Gorilla Dog lives.

He roars as he jumps off the porch and chases me, but I am faster than even the train and I whiz by the donut shop, where I know Harry will be standing at the giant mixer, adding the last of the yeast to the flour. I fly past with my head down.

Blood pounds in my ears. I need an ice cube.

Bells on the donut shop door clang behind me and I soar past the Shop Value and up our driveway, pushing my bike inside the shed, where Harry keeps his old ladder and all his tools, then I rush past Eddie's Barbershop (not stopping for candy or a quick hello) and open the big door to our apartment building. Maybe Harry will believe me when I say it wasn't me on the bike if I am already frying fish sticks and boiling peas.

There is another card from my mum sticking out of the mailbox, you can tell from the tight, thin handwriting. I don't stop, though, and I fly up the stairs, sopping wet, and I don't see the boy in the gigantic wool coat. Of course I plow right into him.

It is a hard hit and we both go flying and the Monopoly game he is holding flips upside down. Red hotels and little green houses scatter everywhere.

"What are you doing just standing in the way like that?" I yell at him, rubbing my knee. I am on edge from the crash and wondering if Harry will catch up to me, and my voice is very loud.

The boy burrows into his coat. His face is thin and pale and his cheekbones stick out like he hasn't had enough to eat. It is hard to tell what the rest of him looks like, because the coat is five sizes too big and reaches to his ankles, but his eyes are a sharp blue.

When Mrs. Salvatore sees me, she yells, "For the love of God, Rosalita, I told you to stay out of that storm." I ignore her because I am watching the boy drop so far into his coat that his ears disappear. "Well, don't just stand there like a clumsy ox," she says. "Help Philippe clean it up."

Oh, fly me to the moon. I scoop up the Monopoly

money as fast as I can, forgetting my bike helmet behind me until it thumps down the stairs at the exact moment the front door opens and my grandpa stomps in with a scowl the size of Saturn.

He figures everything out in about two seconds, I can tell you that.

8

Even my toes sweat. Harry doesn't believe in air conditioners.

My grandpa counts under his breath and tosses his hat on the coffee table and limps to his lazy chair, where he unties his work boots, slips his slippers on, and picks up the newspaper. He whips through the pages too fast.

I hurry into my room—neat and orderly as always (with my papa's old army blanket tucked tight)—and change into a dry shirt and a new pair of shorts. I wipe my springy curls with one of the thread-thin towels that Harry tells me we are going to keep until we can see through them, so stop complaining. Then we have our usual supper with Alex Trebek.

Here's how it works: I cook fish sticks, frozen peas, and fried potatoes on some nights, hot dogs and baked beans on others—the quickest suppers I can think of. Harry wants his jar of pickled hot cherry peppers on the table every night and do not forget the tartar sauce if you want any hearing left. Also, bread and margarine with every meal, you will be sorry if you forget, and make sure there is always coffee brewing. And if you leave the salt off the table you will get the boot right out the door. It's a lot to remember, I can tell you that.

The cat clock over the sink swings its tail, *ticktock*. I pile peas on our plates and snap on the little television that we keep in the kitchen and *Jeopardy!* pops on. Harry winces when he gets up from the lazy chair. My grandpa doesn't want me noticing his gray hair or how his hip bothers him from all the standing he does in front of the donut fryer. I am not supposed to ask why he is limping. If I want to live here, I do not stick my nose in his affairs.

I put three fish sticks on my plate and three on Harry's. I am mighty grateful for the TV. That way we don't have to talk.

Alex Trebek: "Galileo is said to have done gravity experiments by dropping weights from this tower."

Harry sits up, but I rush with "Leaning Tower of Pisa."

Harry grunts, scoops a forkful of fish stick. I wait to eat because a bite of peas might slow me down. The players keep their fingers on the answer buttons. My nose itches. My toes steady themselves.

Alex Trebek: "It's said that Catherine Howard, his fifth wife, still runs screaming through his palace."

"Henry the Eighth!" I scream, just as Harry says, "Hen—"

My toes begin to relax and we go to commercial. I have to pretend to concentrate on the lady washing her kitchen floor with a Swiffer so I won't have to make small talk with Harry. I eat some of my peas. I stab a potato. Harry spreads more margarine on his bread. He shakes salt on his fish. He spoons another lump of tartar sauce. Then he tosses his fork onto his plate and it clangs loudly.

"What I want to know is how can you be thick as a plank?" His brows jab out over his glasses. "Riding out in a storm like that—you could have been killed."

It would be so different with my papa. When things were wrong in my life, he would push the corduroy cushions together in the back of the donut shop and say, "Rosie-Posie, I know something's wrong. You can't fool an old bear like me—now sit and tell me everything."

Augustus would nestle up close and I would feel his warm dog breath on my neck and my papa would stir up a chocolate frappe with whipped cream in summer or a hot cocoa with cinnamon in winter. I'd let out all the hurting things about my mum (like how I really didn't have chicken pox on Mother-Daughter Day, they were purple marker spots so I could stay home, or how she stomped all over the sunflower blooming inside me each time she told me I needed to try harder or I'd never amount to anything).

My papa kept flipping donuts because it was easier to say things when someone wasn't looking straight at you. My papa understood things like that. He knew all about kids and their feelings.

9

"Well?"

Harry takes a loud slurp of coffee and slams the cup down. The table groans. Lights flash, Alex Trebek tells the last-place contestant she is correct about the question I just missed while my ears were buzzing from Harry, and the points add up.

"I told your mother when I took you that I knew nothing about raising a girl. But I do know one thing— you are grounded from that bike."

I jump up; my chair flips over. "For how long?"

"Until you are thirty at least."

I wonder if he can do that. I decide he can't. "But how will I find my dog?"

He tosses his napkin on the table. "I already told you we can't have a big sloppy dog like that living here. Now give it up."

Flea-brained-lout. "I will never give my dog up, not ever."

Harry drums the table. "I never asked for this, Jack," he says under his breath.

Jeopardy! comes back on. Harry snaps the television off. "That was Mrs. Salvatore's new boy you ran over. She wants you to help him." He takes another gulp of coffee.

I clear the table. I throw the fish stick box and two soda cans in the trash, even though Harry tells me to recycle or else. I scour the baking sheet until my fingers cramp. I already mapped out my summer and it is this: each day, every day, I will look for my Augustus, and when I find him, we will spend each day, every day, doing what we love most—being together. "I don't need you to help me make friends."

Harry grunts and puts the jar of pickled hot cherry peppers back in the refrigerator. "This boy—he's a special case. The state asked Mrs. Salvatore to help. And it's not your choice anyway. I've got plans for you all summer long—you *will help* this new boy get settled, plus you can do some cleaning, baking, mending, whatever the heck Mrs. Salvatore wants, and when you're not doing that, you'll be at the donut shop with me. One thing's for sure—I'm locking up that bicycle."

I wheel around. "You can't do that. You can't ground me from my papa's bike."

Harry's ears sizzle. He stomps on the trash can so the lid pops up. "What's this?" he snaps when he sees the cans I wasn't supposed to put in there. "We get five cents apiece for these."

He pulls them out, finds the tuna can I stuffed in there yesterday and also the clam chowder can that now smells like the bottom of the ocean.

"I could skin you alive," he snarls as he digs deeper, and I imagine him reaching the coffee grounds and then feeling beneath to the report card where Miss Holloway listed my grades and wrote that for sixth grade I am going to have Mrs. Barrett (the teacher nobody wants). At the very bottom, in the comments box, she wrote, *Rosalita has had a very difficult year.*

I go back to pot scrubbing. My head throbs. I hold my breath. *Milk-livered-weasel.*

"What's this?" he mutters, standing up behind me, and I hear the wet paper sound of him uncrumpling the folds in my life.

10

After supper on Sunday nights I wait for my mum to call. Here's how it works.

Harry makes sure he is out of the house and off to the donut shop. I ask him doesn't he want to stay and talk to her, too, but he pushes his fishing hat on his head and stomps to the door.

"Then why do I have to?"

He turns around. "Because she's your mother. You *got* to talk to your mother. It won't kill you." Then he slams the door.

I think maybe he is wrong. I think maybe it will.

I sit at the kitchen table, put my feet up, crunch a carrot. I drum my fingers on the table. What I really want to do is get out to the toolshed, pick the lock, pull my bike out, and go find my dog.

I flick on *Jeopardy!*

Alex Trebek: "*In 1865 he said, 'Whenever I hear someone arguing for slavery, I feel a strong impulse to see it tried on him personally.'*"

"Lincoln," I whisper as the phone rings.

"Rosalita?"

"It's Rosie."

"Yes. How are you, Rosalita?" My mum's voice is crisp, clipped.

I shrug.

"How is your summer?"

Silence, except for the drumming of my fingers and the tapping of my toes.

"Rosalita?"

"I'm here."

"I asked you a question."

"I'm fine, same as ever." I roll my eyes.

Silence.

"Very well, then. Put your grandfather on."

"He's not here."

"Again?"

I nod.

"Rosalita?"

"He's at the donut shop."

"Why? It's like he doesn't want to talk with me."

I nod.

"Rosalita, I haven't spoken with him in almost three months."

"Well, you call when he's not here."

"I can't help the time difference from California. I work very long hours, Rosalita. I would appreciate it if you would help me with this."

"It's Rosie."

My mum sighs. "I need to talk with him occasionally, find out how things are going."

"It's not my fault he's not here."

"No, I didn't say it was." My mother is quiet, I hear her breathing. Alex Trebek says: *"A Nebraska brick was a square of prairie turf used to build this type of house."*

I whisper, "Sod."

"What?" my mum says. "What did you say?"

"Nothing," I snap.

"Look, Rosalita, I would like to get more involved in your life."

I imagine her scrubbed and polished, her heels without a single nick. I make a little salute to the air. I am fine here. Not perfect, but at least I have a chance at finding my dog.

"Did you hear me, Rosalita?"

I nod.

"Rosalita? Why won't you answer me? This is so

frustrating." There is quiet for a moment, then: "Robert, this is so upsetting."

Robert is her boyfriend. He is a lawyer, too, and when they aren't working, they host dinner parties and serve caviar and thin crackers on tiny plates.

I hear a muffled voice in the background, then my mum saying, "Rosalita?"

"I'm here. What I really want to know is what did you do with my dog?"

My mum sighs long and slow, like she is letting out fishing line. "You ask me this every single week. Robert, she asks me about that dog every time I call." I hear deep breathing and then: "Rosalita, I already explained to you that I put a sign up at that grocery store across the street and someone came and took the dog. I don't know who it was. Nor do I want to talk about this further."

She pauses, then says, "Rosalita?"

I don't answer.

She sighs and says, "I am making plans to come out so we can discuss your future. Please tell your grandfather I will notify him directly."

Then I hear a click and she is gone.

11

This is what it's like to lose your dog.

You are dull as paint and blank as paper. Your life used to be filled with the lumpiest dog you ever saw— one that pushed out screens and leaped out windows, he was so happy to see you.

He'd run around you, dizzying you up like an old spinning top, and then he'd jump on you and you'd fall and he'd lick your face like you were a piece of sweet butterscotch and he'd turn up his mouth in that funny way of his and you knew he was grinning.

You'd yell at him awful bad for pushing you over like that and for being such a big lug and you'd notice a sad look come in his eyes and you'd feel just terrible. So you'd let him have the fattest pillow on your bed that night, and when he was all snuggled up next to you, he'd sigh and get his Gloaty Gus look on him, like he had the best life of any dog ever, and of course you'd have to hug him because he was right.

The next day—since he had that thing about cats—you'd have to put on his red leash (the one with gold stars all over) and he'd jump around your feet and wrap you up like a bug in a web, so you'd have to let him loose and he'd fly straight for your papa's donut shop, scratching and slobbering all over the door, and wag his tail until your papa gave him a jelly donut with extra jelly.

Then you'd have to wash the windows because your dog made such a mess and your arms ached because dog drool takes such a long time to scrub off.

My dog loved corn on the cob, oatmeal cookies, and me. Sometimes now I dream I am tobogganing behind the donut shop and Augustus jumps on and of course he pushes up front so he can see everything first. I crash—because all I can see is his lumpy behind with his fat tail wagging—and I swallow snow and land in the bushes with my dog on top of me and I laugh because what can be more fun than this?

That's when I wake up in this skinny apartment by the train tracks and see the true way of things: I live with Harry now and I'm half the girl I used to be.

12

The next morning Harry pulls me out of bed or else I would still be there.

"Get up." He stomps over and throws the window up. I moan and burrow under my army blanket.

"You think I got time for this?" he asks. His voice is gravelly in the morning before he has his coffee. He smells like Listerine.

I shrug but he can't see me under my papa's old blanket. I tunnel deeper, to where the Old Spice smell sometimes hides. "There's no school today," I snap. "It's summer."

I wiggle my toes and feel them grin as they wake up. They have forgotten that Harry is making us work all summer. They still think they have all day—every day—to look for my Augustus. I roll over to give them more wiggling room.

"I want you up in two minutes—and dressed." Harry stomps into the kitchen. The coffeepot gurgles.

I pull the fattest pillow over my face as the wind blows and my window rattles. It's cold after all the rain, and the floor shivers. The train rumbles through town, clacking along the tracks, blowing its morning trumpet. I burrow into my blanket. Harry marches back. Even the furniture stands at attention. "You sick?"

I nod but he can't see that. *Sick for my Augustus.* I push my head further under the pillow.

Harry yanks the pillow off. He feels my head. His hands are barnacles on a boat. He pulls the army blanket off and onto the floor. My toes frown. A whiff of Old Spice flits past my nose.

"Up."

"No," I snap, tunneling under my only other pillow, the flat one.

"Get dressed. *Now.*"

I have one plan for today and it is this: break into the toolshed, steal the Blackbird, which Harry locked up—and hunt for my dog.

"I want you in the truck in two minutes," he growls.

It takes only a second for my toes to figure out what Harry is planning—and they shriek right along with me: "I am not going back to where my papa is. I already told you that I am never going again." I search for safe harbor under the pillow.

My grandpa ignores me. "When we get back, you will help Mrs. Salvatore for the rest of the day."

My head pounds. I need an ice cube.

"I won't help her and I won't play with that weird boy. I don't want you to help me make friends."

I can't see Harry, but I can hear him—a bull, snorting mad. All he needs is a ring in his nose.

The wallpaper flinches. "You think I give two cents if you have friends or not?" he roars. "I get enough calls from that teacher saying you took a tailspin this year and how you did this and how you did that and now your grades are in the toilet and nobody likes you. Well, that's your problem."

I don't point out that school was hardly a piece of cake for Harry, either. I roll out from under the pillow. "You can't ground me from my dog."

His chest heaves. I wonder if he will have a stroke. I wish it wasn't my papa who had the stroke. Hornets whirl.

I call my grandpa a *loathsome-toad* and let him think about what it means, although I think he has a pretty good idea. I wrap myself up in my sheet so tight you can't tell if I am a corpse or a girl. My toes hold their breath.

"I'm too old for this. Now *get dressed*. And I don't know who your mother gave that dog to, so don't ask me ever again. *I've had it up to here!*" He yanks the sheet and I unwrap like a jelly roll and flip on the floor.

"Owww." I hold my wrist and check to see if the skin is hanging off.

"Too bad. Now get up." Fire falls from his fingers.

"I can't change with you watching me," I snort.

When he goes, my toes tell me they would like to hear more cusswords, so I call him a *swine-butt* and about a thousand other things, I can tell you that.

13

Harry's truck is the kind you don't worry about much when you bounce over potholes.

Ruts can't make the tailgate rattle any more than it already does. Plus, the windshield wipers are missing rubber, and the seats squeak like gerbils, and when you go over a bump, you tend to hit your head.

I do not want to do this, and I do not look at Harry. The window wants to touch my aching forehead, so I let it.

The lights are off on the JACK'S DONUTS sign, and a piece of cardboard taped to the window says CLOSED. Sam from the pizza shop and the milkman and about a dozen other customers wait on the sidewalk for Harry to open. My grandpa is never late, and he has never missed a day since he took over for my papa. Now he scowls and drives past, drumming his thumb on the steering wheel, and you can see the question mark on everyone's face.

"I already told you I don't think I should have to go." I glower at him.

"Stop talking," he growls.

After my papa had the stroke, I went with Harry to St. Camillus. He warned me about all the sounds—the beeping from the monitors and the pumping of oxygen and the nurses going in and out of the room all the time. And the smells—antiseptic cleaners, mostly, but also the sweet scent of the roses waving me in.

When I walked into my papa's room, the floor sagged under all the sadness. My papa didn't hug me and he didn't read to me and he didn't whisper in my ear the way he did every single night of my whole life when he tucked me in: *I am right here and I will never leave you.*

That was the day my heart jumped right out of my chest and whirling hornets took its place. Now I roar at Harry: "You can't make me."

He ignores me and speeds up. The truck bounces in a pothole and I grab the strap over the door.

"I won't go in there."

He rolls the window down and spits. "Did I say one single thing about going to St. Camillus?"

I erase the surprise off my face. "I thought you were going to make me visit my papa."

"That's for you to decide. This is for me to decide—and it's something I should have done a long time ago."

When Harry turns into the school driveway a few minutes later, he doesn't use his blinker. He pulls right into the principal's spot. The sign frowns.

"What are we doing here?" I can't keep the babyish screech from flying out of my mouth.

I call Harry a *rotten-cabbage-head* under my breath. My knees hold their ears when I shout, "I am not going in. It's summer!"

Harry's eyes pop. "Do you think I want to be here any more than you? I never asked for this. *Not any of it.* Now put a sock in it and get out."

I push my hands in my pockets. Threads snap.

He stomps around and whips open my door. *"Now!"* he bellows.

Harry ignores secretaries. This one is digging through filing cabinets and doesn't look up. Papers and folders shoot for the ceiling, anxious to get out for the summer.

The custodian is here, the one who passes out old candy corn all year long. All the classrooms are dark—chairs on the tables, crates of books on the desks, shades closed. "Isn't there anyone in this whole forsaken place?" Harry grumbles, stopping at one classroom and then the next.

"It's summer," I snort.

"Well, in my day teachers were here all the time."

I let him mutter on. *God's bones.*

14

Harry holds my report card out like it is a dirty fish.

"I don't want you to show anybody *that*," I whine, grabbing for it, but Harry holds it a hundred feet in front of him and marches straight for Mr. Peterson's class at the end of the hall, the only room with any life in it.

Mr. Peterson is the sixth-grade teacher everybody wants. I shove my fists into my pockets and twist. More threads snap.

Opera pours out of his room, and when we step inside, everything glints in the sun. The concrete-block walls are still the color that all the classrooms were when my papa came to read to everyone in first grade: spring-daffodil yellow. Mr. Peterson has pulled off all the blinds and you can see the bird feeders hanging from the cherry tree outside and also the tomato stakes lined up like wooden soldiers in the classroom vegetable patch.

Mr. Peterson is hunched over his desk, writing in a notebook, his pen flying faster than a train rushes in, and he leaves long ribboning tra-la-la trails across the page. Words burst in front of him, and for a few long moments, he doesn't notice us. It's like joy jumps off his hand, flowers bloom. I am hypnotized.

This doesn't happen when I write.

The opera is very loud. Harry's ears twitch.

Once my papa took me to the circus and we held our breath while a tightrope walker inched across the sky. She wobbled quite a bit and fell. That's what opera sounds like—all that wobbling. My head pounds. I scratch the back of my leg with the toe of my sneaker, watching tra-la-las explode like fireworks across Mr. Peterson's notebook.

It's too much for Harry. He marches over and slaps my report card on the desk. Mr. Peterson jumps, and the pen goes quiet.

"She didn't do a darn thing all year!" Harry roars above the opera. "In my day we kept kids back who didn't do anything."

The earth tilts; I grab the desk. I had no idea Harry was even thinking about making me stay back. Grizzlies gnaw at the soft spot behind my eyes.

I make a beeline for the door. Harry grabs my arm. He's got that bull ring in his nose.

Mr. Peterson taps his pen. He pushes his chair back to make more room for his Santa belly.

"Mr. Gillespie, have a seat. Rosalita, how are you?"

"It's Rosie."

Harry stays where he is, snapping his suspenders. Smoke rings circle his ears.

Mr. Peterson flips my report card from one side to the other, concentrating on the spot where Miss Holloway wrote about my terrible year. After a while, he says, "We do not repeat grades in this school, Mr. Gillespie, except in extreme cases, and that's not the situation here." The grizzlies in my head begin to relax.

He turns to me. "Rosie, your language arts grades are particularly low. You don't like to read?"

I do. I *love* to read—especially my *World Book*—and I *really really love* being read to, as long as it's my papa doing the reading. If I stacked all the books my papa read to me, they would fill this room—and Miss Holloway's, too.

15

This is how I turned out to be a kid who loves reading.

My mum left for California to make something of herself before I even had my first birthday. She hated all the sand and grit that clung to our town like sugar. She also hated snow.

My papa was heartbroke. Harry had to yell at him in that gruff Marines voice that makes even the kitchen table stand straighter, and after a while my papa pulled himself together and opened the donut shop.

He learned to be mama/papa and bought me oodles of books and read them to me in my bedroom under the eaves. We had reading celebrations with donuts and frappes when we finished a book and we baked a six-layer chocolate cake (with raspberry filling) when I read my first fat chapter book.

I was the youngest kid in the history of our town ever to get a library card—or so my papa bragged to everyone at the donut shop. We kept pages and pages of lists of all the books we read, and when we discovered *The World Book*, we started making up cusswords.

I may hate to do math sheets and write prompts for Miss Holloway, and I may hate everything she had to say all year long, but I love everything about our town library—the smell and the computers all lined up and turned on and Mrs. Moore behind the counter ready to point out a book on some North Pole explorer you never heard of and the hopeful feeling you have in your heart when you open a book for the first time and the plastic cover crackles in your hands.

My papa loved it all, too, and we measured our stacks to see whose was taller. (Usually mine.)

One day a big, lumpy, unwashed, unwanted, unloved bear-dog ran up the library steps and jumped on me as I was walking down. I tumbled, my books flew, and I landed on my ankle the wrong way and saw stars.

The dog licked my nose and I yelled at him awful bad, but then I noticed a gloaty grin on his face like he was about to get the best life of any dog ever, and of course I had to hug him because he was right.

16

Harry does not believe in feelings or in beating around the bush.

"In my day we'd say she didn't have the sense of a chicken," my grandpa roars. Mr. Peterson's desk stands straighter. "If you won't keep her back, I want a tutor, then—make her do the work she didn't do all year long."

Harry pauses to look at all the bookshelves that sag under the weight of too many books, and also at all the stacks that pop up all over the floor like anthills. I see him make up his mind, and then he tells Mr. Peterson: "You can tutor her."

Blood pounds in my ears. My belly sinks as it realizes what this will mean for my plan of getting my dog back before my mum sticks her nose in my future. My papa would never make me have a teacher all summer long. "I don't need a tutor," I snort.

Harry glares. All the books around the room consider restacking themselves. I need an ice cube.

Mr. Peterson clicks his pen. "I don't have time to tutor anyone, Mr. Gillespie. I have six children of my own. This is summer vacation."

"Look, I'm just asking you to knock some sense into that thick skull of hers. I don't care how you do it. A few times over the summer—at the donut shop, where I can keep an eye on her." Harry nods to the pictures of Mr. Peterson's children. "With all those mouths to feed, no doubt you could use the cash."

Mr. Peterson hems and haws. I humph. If Harry has so much money, why doesn't he buy me snacks that I like or new towels without holes or maybe an air conditioner? I open my mouth to say this, but Mr. Peterson asks, "Do you have a journal?"

I don't believe in journals, especially not ones like Miss Holloway gave us: embarrassing little notebooks with pink daisies and smiley faces and litters of purring kittens crawling all over. I ball my fists into cement mixers and twist them deep in my pockets.

Mr. Peterson reaches into his drawer and pulls out a black-and-white-speckled notebook. "Never mind, we'll use this." He picks up his pen, and before I can tell him what I really think about keeping a journal, he tra-la-las all over this one, too. Then he says, "This is how I'll tutor you, with a notebook. And if you give it a chance, I will talk to the principal about transferring you into my class."

I open the cover a sliver.

"Not here, not here. I want you to think about it when you get home. You need to be alone to jump into an idea like this. You need to sink under the waves, swim around for a while, let the idea seep in your skin, see what it has to say to you."

Harry grunts. He holds out his hand for Mr. Peterson to shake. It better be strong, because Harry doesn't believe in wet trout. Then my grandpa steers me out the door. "What kind of nonsense is going on in this school, anyway?"

Prune-faced idiot, I say to myself as I walk toward his truck.

Dunce-head.

Surly-cow.

17

I open my window, wedge myself through the skinny space, and climb onto the fire escape. I bring the black-and-white-speckled notebook with me.

My Gloaty Gus never knew this place. He would have loved how you can perch yourself two stories up on an iron ladder that sways like straw when the wind gusts down from the sandpits. Especially, Augustus would have loved how you can get away from Harry out here.

I open the notebook.

There is a loud crash in Mrs. Salvatore's apartment. Paulie yells at Francesca for hiding his turtle and then Francesca is howling and Sarah, the oldest, is screaming will everybody be quiet so she can just read her book and then Mrs. Salvatore is banging something, probably a pot, against the kitchen table and yelling: "You stop that, Francesca, you hear?" And then when Paulie starts wailing, Mrs. Salvatore bellows, "Night and day you two are going to be the death of me. What did I do to the good God in heaven to deserve this?"

I pull my springy curls back, take a deep breath, and wonder how *do* you dive into a notebook and swim around for a while? All of a sudden I very much want to feel Mr. Peterson's tra-la-las.

I flip to the first page. If Augustus could write, it would look like Mr. Peterson's writing—big, bold, sloppy letters that have no manners and could use an obedience class.

> Fill these pages with your story, Rosie, and if you do, I will share mine.
>
> P.S. I hope my story won't make you ill. There's going to be a lot of throwing up—enough to fill a sand truck.
>
> P.P.S. (I will read your story only if you want me to.)

I slam the notebook shut and squeeze myself back through the chipped window frame and tumble into my skinny bedroom, where my army blanket forgets how to smell like Old Spice. There's enough grit on my dresser to write my name on the top.

I shove the notebook deep in my bottom drawer. This isn't tra-la-las. This is work, more work than Miss Holloway ever asked for, so much work that I could never finish it—and *find my dog*—before my mum comes.

I was wrong about the tra-la-las and everything else that I thought Mr. Peterson was writing in my notebook.

Plague-sore.

Canker-face.

Goat-bellied-mule.

18

Shoot me, please.

This is how I feel two minutes after I start playing Monopoly with the boy in the gigantic wool coat.

"I am not going to be the iron," I snap, uncramping my leg because we are sitting on the floor. Already I am at the boiling point.

They don't even sell Monopoly games with irons in them anymore—that tells you how old this board is. Plus, the money is crumpled and the deeds are bent and frayed at the edges. My face is hot, my head aches. The boy's bedroom is smaller than mine, and the air conditioner rattles and bumps and keeps shutting down. I pull the ice cube out of the baggie in my pocket and rub it on my brow. Then I suck on it, holding out my hand. "Give me the dog."

The boy shakes his head and sweat sprays onto his coat, which looks like it came from the bottom of the bin at the Church of Our Risen Lord thrift shop. He tosses me the shoe.

I let it drop on the board. It rolls over to St. James Place. "I am *always* the dog," I hiss. This is a lie because I never play Monopoly, but if I did, I would be the dog. I pull my springy curls off my neck and lean into the air conditioner when it clicks on. I lift my arms and let the cool blow under.

Philippe shrugs, picks up the ship, and holds it out.

I shake my head. "I'm not playing if I can't be the dog."

The only things not covered by the heavy wool coat are his eyes and his thin nose and the curls on top of his head, which are so pale they remind me of the donut filling Bavarian cream. He shrugs and puts the ship back in the box. "That's okay. I like playing by myself better." His voice is grainy and scruffy like when you walk on the boardwalk at the beach.

"You *can't* play Monopoly by yourself," I snort. I pull off my flip-flops and sit on my heels, sinking my toes into the blue shaggy rug, searching for a cool spot. Empty soda cans burst out the top of a garbage bag under the window. Harry would have a bug.

I wipe the sweat off my face. Philippe ignores me and

carefully sets the Chance cards on the board and stacks the Community Chest pile. He has already fixed himself a bowl of cereal, which he pulls out from under his bed. He eats several spoonfuls without offering me any, and milk dribbles down his thin chin. When he finishes, he pulls a cereal box from under the bed and a quart of milk from behind his pillow.

If you knew Mrs. Salvatore, your mouth would be wide as a door, I can tell you that. Her kitchen looks the way kitchens in television commercials look. There are seven people living in this apartment—including Mr. Salvatore, who you never see because he hauls trucks long-distance—and you could eat mashed potatoes right off the floor without dusting them off, that's how everything sparkles. The sink is bleached and shined, the inside of her coffee cups are white as Easter lilies, and there's no sticky jelly prints on the refrigerator. When your head is cluttered up with too much going wrong, it's good to be someplace neat and orderly like Mrs. Salvatore's kitchen.

"What are you doing?" I am incredulous.

Philippe watches me nervously as he fills his bowl a second time. "Want some?" He looks back and forth from me to the door.

"Of course not, I already ate breakfast." No one ever had to tell me not to eat in my bedroom—some things you just know. I get the feeling this boy might need a few lessons on how to get on in this world.

He pours another bowl. This is his third. I try and think back if I ever ate three bowls of cereal at once.

"Are you going to tell?" he whispers.

I dig my toes deeper into the cool spot, where they are happier. "Can I be the dog?"

Philippe scrapes the last of the cereal from the bottom of the bowl with his tongue and hides everything under the bed. He hands me the race car. "I have to be the dog," he whispers.

I could wring his neck. Instead, I remind myself that I need to get out of here quickly so I can pick the lock on the toolshed, steal my bike, and hunt for my dog. Already the sun is high.

I stuff a pillow under me and try to relax my toes. They are losing patience. "Playing Monopoly by yourself is the stupidest idea ever," I say, getting back to that subject. "How do you not cheat?"

"Why would I cheat?" He rolls his eyes. "I play with Teddy Roosevelt. Why would I want to cheat with him?"

I push the pillow away, sit up. My mouth is open again. "He's dead."

Philippe shrugs and hands out the money to himself and to an imaginary player on the other side. He leaves me out.

Shoot me.

After a moment of watching him, I grab the shoe out of the box and pull Teddy Roosevelt's money over to me.

I rub my hands together so hard they sizzle and I throw the dice. I roll a perfect pair of snake eyes.

19

This is how you pick a lock.

First, you need two jumbo paper clips. These aren't easy to find in our apartment because Harry is out of practice about school supplies.

I have to dig to the bottom of all our kitchen drawers to find two. I straighten the first clip. This will be the pick. *The World Book of Unbelievable and Spectacular Things* says that's all there is to the first one.

For the second, the tension wrench, things are more complicated. I straighten two of the curves in the wire. Then, with a pair of Harry's pliers, I squeeze the last bend together, creating a double thickness. I twist that into a right angle about half an inch down. Next, I twist the bottom where the wire is a single thickness, to make it look like a piece of licorice. *The World Book* says I should now have two tools that look like this: *L I*

Out at the toolshed, I hold the wires up, pushing at them with my finger. They wobble because Harry bought the cheap ones at Walmart.

The World Book of Unbelievable and Spectacular Things says I need to force the tension wrench into the slit at the bottom of the padlock to wedge things open. Then I push in the other clip and wiggle to move the tumblers. I do this. Nothing happens.

I lift the padlock and look into the slit. I push the bent wire in, but this time I do it harder. I stick the straight wire in and wiggle it around. Nothing happens.

The sun pastes my springy curls to my neck. I grind my teeth and try again, but it is windy today and grit flies down from the sandpits and gums up the works. I trace my finger all around the place in the lock where my wires are supposed to go.

The phone rings in our apartment. I bet it is my mum calling to have that talk with Harry, but—ha ha— my grandpa isn't home. I snort and shove the tension wrench back in, closer to the top. I push it with my thumb to try and open things up. Then I push in the straight wire, wiggling it twice as much as I did before.

Nothing happens.

Louse-head. Fish-breath. Mealy-mouth. I cuss at Harry and the lock at the same time.

This gives Mrs. Salvatore and her big nose a chance

to get right up behind me without me noticing. She's got her laundry basket, and all her foster children stand quietly behind her (I swear they've never been this silent before; my toes can hardly believe it), and then the peacefulness is too much for everyone and Francesca wedges Paulie's fingers apart so she can get at whatever he's hiding in his hand, and he yelps. Sarah, the oldest, has a book and the baby in her arms and then the baby turns beet red and screams and she drops the book and Philippe burrows in his coat. I would like to ask him where is his best friend, Teddy Roosevelt, but then Paulie screams about how Francesca is going to hurt his turtle and Mrs. Salvatore pushes him behind her, and this gives Francesca a chance to step closer to me.

"What's she doing to that lock?"

That's all Mrs. Salvatore needs to start sniffing like an old hound dog again.

20

I walk five times as fast as Philippe and every time I have to stop and wait for him, I breathe in a gush of hot dusty grit. I pull my shirt over my nose.

"It's hot enough to fry an egg—can't you walk faster?" My voice is machete-sharp under my shirt.

Philippe treads a dozen paces behind me, the buckle from his coat clacking along the hot pavement. His head is the only thing not covered by the coat. It's like I'm walking with a rolled-up rug.

We are headed to the hardware store because Mrs. Salvatore needs a new mop. Plus, she figured out I was up to something with the lock.

"Night and day your grandfather works his tail off to feed you, and this is how you treat him?"

I snort. I don't think we are talking about the same Harry.

* * *

This is the Harry I know: On that first day after I moved in, all I found in his cupboards were soggy saltines and graham crackers that were floppy as worms. And who knew how long the can of tuna had been sitting on the shelf with its label missing (and was it even tuna?), plus the mayonnaise was sour-lemon-smelling and it made me crabby to even look at it.

There were margarine sticks instead of real butter, and all the spices in the rack were packed in little cans with rusted covers. I read in *The World Book of Unbelievable and Spectacular Things* that folks in the Middle Ages thought rust would jump from one piece of metal to another like fleas if you weren't careful. I told this to Harry and I said it really snippy because cornflakes made my belly ache (my papa gave me brown sugar oatmeal) and I was starving half to death and a girl as skinny as me needs three meals a day of *food she likes*, plus good snacks, and he just said, "Humph," and opened a can of corned beef and put half on my plate and there was no mustard and this riled me up even more, I can tell you that. He ate a lot of canned sardines and fried potatoes and his favorite was Spam sandwiches. I was bad-tempered and weak with hunger for a week, until I took matters into my own hands.

My *World Book* says:

> *Wait for a distraction, or create one yourself,*
> *but by all means never attempt to pickpocket*
> *without one. Children on the streets of London*
> *knew how two hundred years ago, and you need*
> *to understand this if you are to be any good.*

My papa told me when we were reading this chapter that this was horrible advice—especially if you want to be a good person—but he doesn't have to live with Harry now. I do.

Philippe and I aren't even halfway to the hardware store when he picks a grimy Pepsi can off the culvert on Main Street and puts it in his pocket.

He reaches into the trash bucket outside the dentist's office, pulls out two empty cans of Mountain Dew, and puts them in the other pocket.

My toes sizzle to the tops of my flip-flops. *"What are you doing?"*

He ignores me and searches through the trash bucket by the Rockdale Savings & Trust.

When I get to the big house where Gorilla Dog lives, I race past. I am so far ahead of Philippe I don't bother to warn him.

21

Gary's Hardware is a little shoe box of a building at the edge of the rail tracks.

When the train screeches through town, the whole place trembles and the racks of ROCKDALE: WHERE FOUNDATIONS ARE BUILT key chains and paperweights and plastic gravy boats tumble to the floor. You would think someone would have sense enough to move the racks.

The old cowbell on the door clanks when I walk in, and Mrs. Gary looks up from her crossword puzzle.

It's not your usual hardware store, like Home Depot or Lowe's. Here everything is pushed against something else. A barrel filled with nails and boxes of daffodil bulbs are shoved against a wall of wrenches, hammers, light sockets, and wood glue. There are crochet hooks, knitting needles, and embroidery hoops hanging on a wall beside a big drum of dog biscuits, painter's canvas, and garden hose. There is a whole wall for cleaning supplies: Windex, Pine-Sol, vacuum cleaner bags, Swiffers, water buckets, and Mop & Glo.

I hurry past a stack of cast-iron fry pans, glass casserole dishes, a cluster of wooden spoons, turkey basters, and salt and pepper shakers, but instead of going to the aisle with the mops, I stop at the shelf of junk food, which might be unusual merchandise for a hardware store, but not this one.

Harry says we don't have money to buy Yodels and Yankee Doodles and those little cupcakes frosted with pink coconut icing—if I want something sweet, eat a donut. This might leave your mouth watering, if you haven't eaten a donut every day for your entire life.

"What do you want, Rosalita?" Mrs. Gary asks me as I look through a box of Ring Pops.

"A new mop," I say, looking up, snorting to myself that Philippe hasn't even made it inside yet. I decide on the box of Jolly Rancher sticks and position myself.

I look for cans to topple to create a distraction. My papa says in my head: *This is a very bad idea.*

"You won't find mops in that aisle," Mrs. Gary says. "That would be by the Windex, next aisle over." She gets up and walks around the counter.

When Philippe finally opens the door, I am trying to

quickly decide between a watermelon and a green apple stick.

The bell over his head clangs. Mrs. Gary's husband, who reads the newspaper all day, looks up from the wheelchair he's been in since the Vietnam War. I quickly choose the watermelon stick and stuff it in my pocket.

Philippe is such a sight to behold that Mrs. Gary stops midstep.

This makes Philippe stiffen like a starched sheet. He locks his eyes on the sliver of black high-top that sticks out from under his coat. Somehow a maple leaf got stuck in his hair.

He looks up for a second and sees all of us watching him, and his face gets so red it looks as if he has been slapped, and he clamps his teeth shut. It's like he straps a muzzle on so tight he couldn't talk even if you pinched him. He sinks further into his coat and accidentally brushes against a display of charcoal briquettes and lighter fluid and marshmallows and graham crackers and Hershey bars and everything you need to toast s'mores.

"My goodness, he's going to tip it over," Mrs. Gary says, hurrying around the counter.

This makes Philippe burrow inside his coat like he is diving under a wave.

Only the tops of his eyes and his pale curls show. *This*

is one weird kid. I notice a display of geranium beauty soap and I push a bar into the back of my waistband so I don't have to smell like Harry's Irish Spring.

"Careful!" Mrs. Gary yells, and I jump, but she is rushing past the tomato stakes and garden wire toward Philippe, her hands waving.

This is too much for Philippe and he backs up and the whole s'mores pyramid sways, and before Mrs. Gary can get to it, everything topples to the floor.

"Don't touch it, don't touch anything!" Mrs. Gary bellows. Mr. Gary wheels around the counter.

Philippe trips over a can of lighter fluid and slips and an empty can of Mountain Dew rolls out of his pocket. Mrs. Gary raises her arm like she is going to hit him. Mr. Gary picks up a broom.

Do something, I hear my papa say in my head, or maybe it is me saying it, it is hard to tell. Watching Philippe feels like seeing a puppy about to be kicked. I grab his coat, haul him up, and hurry us out the door. I don't bother checking to see if Gorilla Dog is waiting or not.

22

"I saw your grandpa locking up your bike," says Cynthia, the girl from the attic apartment above us who thinks I am her friend (but I am not).

She pops up behind me while I am scrubbing fingerprints off the donut case. A Barbie sticks out of each front pocket of her shorts. She is wearing the same tie-dyed shirt she wears nearly every day of the week and she sips from a can of grape soda. Her lips are stained. She scratches.

"Did he lock it up for the whole summer?" Cynthia's voice has a hummingbird flutter in it.

"No, of course he didn't lock it up for the whole summer. Keep your nose out of my business, Cynthia." I spray more Windex, seething because I am in such a hurry to get my chores done.

Cynthia coughs and wipes her hand on the donut case.

Hornets whirl. "I said *go away!*"

"But I don't have anybody to play with. I never have anybody to play with. My mama says I should play with you because you are alone all the time. Even Miss Lindsey said I should play with you."

Miss Lindsey is the third-grade teacher who reads to her students every afternoon after lunch and makes them put their heads on their desks so they will relax. I outgrew teachers like her a long time ago.

I pull the ice cube out of the baggie in my pocket and dab my forehead. Cynthia edges closer. She flips her hair out of her face, and when she does, her hair flops over in a thick clump and you can see the nest underneath from where she doesn't brush. On the bus I sometimes have to sit behind her, and when you are close, you can see how she just sort of combs the top of her hair over everything and pats it in place. It makes me wonder why her mother doesn't take better care of her. It feels good to think bad things about someone else's mum for a change.

"But I just wanted to ask you to come over and play. What's wrong with that? Or I could help. I can wash things. I like to do things like that. I do all the cleaning at our house and I never break a dish or anything."

I squirt my bottle of Windex and listen to the glass yelp about all the ammonia. I scowl. "Go away, Cynthia." It is infuriating she is pestering me when I am in such a hurry to find my dog.

Harry already made me brew five hundred pots of coffee and fill ten thousand jelly donuts. My bike is still locked up and I hear it calling for me.

The new conditions of my life are these: I will work out front at the donut shop. (Harry does not believe in small talk or chatter and customers give him a headache.)

If I don't want to do that, I can help Mrs. Salvatore and be friends with her new boy—which, after the Monopoly game and the trip to the hardware store, I wouldn't do in a million years.

At night I will jump in that notebook and swim around for a while, or whatever the heck it is that I am supposed to do. (Harry tells me in his day you didn't write your life story, you lived it.)

Once a week Mr. Peterson will stop by the donut shop and see how I am getting on. In the meantime, I will not look for my dog or talk about my dog or even think about my dog. Harry has had it up to here.

If I do not choose to come around to my grandpa's way of thinking, I can fry donuts in the back of the shop until the cows come home. Even the walls sweat back there.

23

The train rumbles through town, and when it's gone, there's that emptying, that blank quiet you get before snow.

Cynthia grabs my arm.

I look up quickly as Swanson, her hunting hat pulled low, her gray eyes on me, walks through the door of the donut shop.

I gulp, wondering if she's here to tell Harry how far I rode in the storm. I try and shake Cynthia off me but she won't let go.

"She shoots squirrels, Rosie. She's got a wolf nose—do you know what wolves do to kids?" Cynthia squeezes tighter. "They tear them apart."

Coffee cups crash inside me, teapots fly. "Cynthia, I said go *away*!"

Swanson holds a wicker basket and points to the donuts without looking at me. I glance back for Harry, because he doesn't believe in free handouts, and I know that is what she's expecting.

The customers sitting at the counter stop talking because you don't see Swanson every day. Avery Taylor hoots and climbs out of the back booth and strolls over, his friends snickering behind him.

When Swanson refuses to look at him, he whispers, "What's wrong, you don't like me?"

Harry is in the back room and doesn't see this or else he would send Avery Taylor flying out the door. No one else says a word. No one ever says anything to Avery Taylor because of the hockey team. Other than donuts and coffee, the antidote to all the grit flying around here is a fast game on cold ice.

My papa would send Avery Taylor packing. "Leave." I point to the door.

He turns, astonished that I am daring to talk to him. He steps forward, ready to pick a fight.

"Get out!" I roar this time, and Harry stomps out from the back. The chairs stand straighter.

"You got mush for brains?" Harry's voice is a low growl. "My granddaughter said to get out."

My heart swells the teeniest bit as I watch Harry. You can see Avery Taylor deciding if he wants to take on my grandpa, but he doesn't, and when he storms out, the bells on the door clap that he is gone. Swanson reaches into the deep pocket of her coat, pulls something out, and puts it on the counter, covering it with her hand.

One thing about Swanson, she never pays with cash. It's always a few turnips from her garden or a bunch of pie apples from her orchard or a dozen chicken eggs from her barn. Cynthia groans. "It's a knife."

When I finally shake Cynthia off me, Swanson lifts her hand. An old silver bracelet with a missing jewel sits on the counter.

"Wow, can I have it?" Cynthia asks, edging closer.

After I get Swanson's donuts packed, she nods to me and pushes the bracelet toward Cynthia, who jumps and grabs it. "Oh boy, I always wanted one of those," she says (plus a million other happy things like that). Then Swanson walks out and the bells on the door skip behind her. The milkman turns to his buddies. "She's got a big bear of a dog out there, bites my wheels, an absolute pain in the neck—reminds me of Gillespie's old dog."

I drop my cleaning cloth, I can tell you that.

Five minutes later I am so busy stabbing my paper clips into the padlock on our toolshed that I don't hear Philippe walk up behind me.

"Thank you," he says, startling me, making me jump.

"No one ever helps me like you did at that hardware store."

I push the clips in the lock. After I poke for about a million years, Philippe comes up closer. The heat rolls off his coat.

"Do you want me to pick that?" he asks.

I scowl at the thin boy with the hair the color of Bavarian cream. I scoff: "What do you know about locks?"

Very quietly, in a voice soft as feathers, he whispers, "My mama taught me how."

24

The dusk whines with mosquitoes by the time Philippe gets the lock open and I fix my wobbling wheel and fly past the American Legion, where Harry is playing cards. An old wooden sawhorse props the front door open to let out the cigar smoke.

Harry deals, *snap snap snap*. He looks up for an instant. *God's bones.*

I pedal faster. The flashlight bounces in the Blackbird's wire basket and the kickstand is all peeved that we have to go anywhere at this time of night and it slips down and scrapes against the pavement and I have to knock some sense into it with my foot.

I turn my headlight on. My papa always told me it's hard enough to ride during the day in our town because of all the grit on the road. I steer my tires through sand, feel the wind whip my face. I can hardly believe my mum would give my Augustus to someone like Swanson. I race onto the next road and soar down the next, pedaling furiously up the first hill for as long as I can before I have to stand. My back wheel slips. A car roars past and spits gravel at my goggles. Sharp bits chisel my face.

It's chilly this time of night. My shoulders tell me I could surely use Philippe's wool coat right about now and, by the way, why am I all alone and why didn't I bring a friend and *how come no one knows where I am?*

By the time I get out to the east part of town, where Swanson lives, it is dark. There are no streetlights because no one else lives out here, and grit crackles under my wheels. Something scurries across the road up ahead. My headlight flickers and I shut it off. My brain hooks into all the things I shouldn't be thinking about when I am pedaling along a dark road by myself. It's like a movie in my head—Swanson shooting squirrels and skinning them, Swanson racing so fast she can catch you no matter how fast you run, and all the other things Cynthia and the kids at school say she does, like curdle milk just by looking at it. I yell at myself to stop, but my head keeps picturing that bone face and that wolf nose and it's like trying not to look at a squashed turtle in the road. Already I have a headache.

No one knows where I am.

I turn onto the road leading to Swanson's farm, wondering how I am going to get my Gloaty Gus away from there, kicking myself for forgetting to bring a rope to lead him home.

Three-quarters of the way up Swanson's steep hill, I get off and push. I try the headlight again and it glows for a few seconds and then flicks off. A chilly gust pushes sand in my cheek.

No one knows where I am.

I climb back on my bike and start down the hill, dragging my sneakers, my heart hammering in my chest. The train rumbles along tracks that run through Swanson's far fields, and it picks up speed as it goes, hurrying to towns without all the grit.

The Blackbird has the natural feeling it wants to give up the slow stuff and fly—who needs brakes anyway?— but I try and explain as we bump ahead in the dark how you need to be a little careful about rushing toward Swanson, even if the true-blue friend of your soul is waiting for you there.

I steer around the rocks in the road with big snaking swirls. My back wheel slides in the sand, and as I try to keep from slipping, Harry's flashlight flies out of the basket and rolls into the gully on the side of the road.

I yell at myself for not holding tighter.

Harry will have a fit.

25

My plan is simple: I will take a few minutes to wrap my arms around my Gloaty Gus and sink my face in his warm clumpy dog fur and feel his heart beating, then we will rush off into the night together like they do in Harry's old movies—something like that.

I hide the Blackbird in the pricker bushes at the bottom of Swanson's driveway and step into the shadows.

Under the moon, the pitched roof of her little house points sharply to the stars. A jagged picket fence rushes across the front yard and a hanging bulb casts a hazy light over her porch. Loud television voices scratch through the window screens. A barn stands off to the side, tall as a fire tower. Cynthia says it's the place Swanson shoots squirrels. I told her that doesn't make any sense—if she *did* shoot squirrels, she'd do it in the woods—but

Cynthia said no, all the bad things happen in that barn, that's what her mama says. It's hard to believe anything Cynthia's mother says about anything.

Swanson's front door is open—only a wire screen stands between me and the inside. The wind picks up and I pull my shirt over my nose. A dozen bird feeders clack and spin like ghosts in the trees above me. My *World Book* says anytime you even *think* about ghosts, one of them is probably right beside you, nuzzling up to your ear.

I would do anything for my dog, even this.

My heart asks what am I waiting for; my brain says not so fast. *No one knows where I am.* I take a deep running breath and fly up the driveway, pounding the hard dirt, keeping to the shadows, my toes complaining the whole way about the stones drilling their way up through the holes in my sneakers. I stumble on a tree root, yelp, and plow into some thorny wild roses, falling, rolling, slicing my cheek. This is crazy—anyone would think this is crazy. If Harry knew, he would have a cow.

The television turns down—then footsteps and floor creaking. The screen door opens and Swanson steps out, standing only a few feet away from the spot where I am hiding. I am soaked with sweat, faint with heat, weak with the possibility of finding my dog. A small army of mosquitoes finds my ears as I hold my breath and try hard to think what to do next.

After a moment, the screen door slaps shut, the television turns up, and I crawl out from under the roses. I test the first porch step with my foot. When you are thin as an eel, you don't make much noise. I climb up another step and the next until I reach the front door, then feel my way along the dim light, tiptoeing through the shadows.

A baseball game is on, seventh-inning stretch from the sound of it. Harry loves baseball and now I know all about batting averages and pitching speeds, which are the last things I ever wanted to know about.

I step around a metal milk box, scoot down beneath a window, and carefully pull myself up.

It is not easy to wake my very bad dog Augustus. When he would stretch out on my bed—with his head on my pillow, snuggled up next to me—you could put a hunk of roast beef (with gravy) in front of his nose and he wouldn't stir. Sometimes a noise would get him to prick up an ear, but usually he slept through everything, except of course the smell of cat or the milkman roaring by. "That dog's not a dog," my papa would say. "He's a bear. He'd sleep all winter if he could."

This isn't true. Still, if my Augustus is sleeping beside Swanson's television, I am going to have a devil of a time waking him up.

Through the window, I can see Swanson sitting on the couch with a bowl of popcorn on her lap. There's a fireplace with an old shotgun hanging on the mantel and an iron-black pail heaped with ashes, but there's no dog. Could the milkman be so stupid he got it wrong? I swoop down, crawl to another window, and pop up to look in that one, then another and another.

Blood roars in my ears. Didn't the milkman say *just like Gillespie's old dog*? I pull myself back up for another look at Swanson.

This time she gasps. I jump back, knocking the milk box off the porch.

She can catch you no matter how fast you run.

I jump off the porch and mad-gallop across the grass, keeping to the shadows. Surely I can run fast enough to reach the Blackbird before Swanson catches me, but I plow into a bird feeder, sending it spinning, and have to throw myself on the ground as the beam from Swanson's flashlight rolls over my back. I shiver from the smooth feel of it and try to cast off the parade of thoughts that marches through my mind—squirrels, curdled milk, dark creepy barns.

No one knows where I am.

I am up, off, crawling like a baby across the yard, half in the bushes, half out, my curls catching in the thorny roses. I try to give the barn a wide berth but Swanson is walking fast and there is protection in the deep shadows cast out by its bony frame.

When I get up close, I trip on a tree root branching across my path like a thick ropy vein and I knock my knee against it and cry out, howling like a dog before I catch myself.

And then—when I am not expecting anything but Swanson's flashlight to sweep over me again—a loud booming bark rises from deep inside the barn: a glorious hallelujah that I would know anywhere.

My Gloaty Gus.

26

I freeze the way you do in statue tag. Swanson's flash-light sweeps closer, waving back and forth over the dry stubble lawn, but I can't seem to move my legs, *I can't move my legs*, and my very bad dog Augustus barks again and again from inside the barn and my heart thumps out of my chest to go find him.

I roll into a spread of prickly juniper bushes, cuss at the new cuts on my cheeks. Swanson's flashlight bounces over the grass, spreading light through the dark the way a lighthouse sends beams across the sea. My Gloaty Gus howls inside the barn.

I roll a little further and wedge against a rough tree trunk. Swanson's footsteps crunch in the dry grass. A mosquito lands on my neck. I flick it away without mak-ing a sound. I hold my breath as Swanson comes closer, let it out slowly when I am near to fainting, then take in more air in tiny little puffs. Crickets sing. Swanson is so close I can hear her breathing. The beam from her flashlight bounces over my sneakers. I practice being dead.

I press myself into the ground, pretending I am falling all the way to China. After a very long while, Swanson turns back for the house. I suck in deep gasping breaths, and when the dizziness fades, I crawl out from under the bush and run for the barn.

A heavy padlock hangs from the doors. I wiggle it, pick it up, and try to open it, but it is snapped tight. *Why would she bolt my dog in like this?* I heave the padlock against the doors. This makes my very bad dog Augustus bark like an insane nut: *Why aren't you rescuing me?*

The porch door squeaks open again and I rush to the shadows on the side of the barn, trying to think of a plan, while my dog wails inside. I flatten myself to the rough boards and edge around the back. It is very dark. I wish I had the flashlight. Augustus roars.

There's a small window, higher than I can reach. I look around for something to stand on—a log, a chair, a milk bucket. But already it's too late. Swanson is walking her slow shuffle across the lawn. I press my cheek against the wood siding as my very bad dog Augustus scratches and whines against the inside wall and our hearts nearly touch.

The dumb thing to do now would be to get caught; the smart thing to do would be to rush into the woods and come back with help. I hear my papa telling me, *You need patience in this life, Rosie.*

I tap at the wall that separates us, whispering to my Gloaty Gus that I will be back, and it breaks my heart to leave him in the barn where Cynthia says all the bad things happen, but as Swanson pulls at the big barn doors out front, I decide I have no choice but to fly into the woods.

When I finally pull my bike out of the prickers, I can see Swanson still sweeping her flashlight closer, closer.

I jump on the Blackbird and begin pedaling, but the chain is clanking and I have to climb off and fix it.

The moon is high as I finally fly toward home.

My dog's barking fills my heart.

God's bones, it is a miracle.

27

Main Street is empty when I rush the Blackbird into town. The American Legion is shut up and the donut shop is closed. Harry's truck is gone.

I push my bike into the toolshed and run up the steps of our apartment building and unlock our door.

Inside, everything is dark, except for the light over the kitchen sink. The toilet runs, the pipes clang. My grandpa's bedspread is Marines-tight, and as I look in, the numbers on the clock on his dresser flip to 11:15.

There's a note from Harry on my bed:

OUT LOOKING FOR YOUR SORRY BUTT.

He wrote with such a heavy hand he ripped the paper. My chest burns, my head pounds.

I jump under the sheets and pull the army blanket up, not bothering to find the Old Spice smell. The little green clock that Harry gave me ticks on my dresser. Harry used it when he was a boy and it's as dented as my bike. I roll one way and then the other. My nerves twist.

It is almost midnight when Harry stomps up the stairs. He flicks on the light in the hall and stops at my door. I make my breathing deep and regular like I am sleeping. I snore softly, trying not to overdo it.

My grandpa stands in my doorway, his breathing wheezy and old. After a very long time, he says, "I never asked for this, Jack. Not any of it." Then he walks away.

My clock ticks for another half hour before my nerves untangle and I doze off, and just before I do, I hear my papa in my head: *Your grandpa came looking for you, didn't he? He came looking for you just like I would have done.*

PART II

28

On the terrible night I lose my papa, my feet ache from standing and I shift my weight to give one foot and then the other a rest.

The palm of my right hand cramps from pumping strawberry jelly and Bavarian cream. I remember that, and also how my papa pulls the donuts from the sizzling oil and hangs them like life jackets on a line. Then he lifts our favorite book from the shelf.

You don't have to tell me twice, and you don't have to tell Augustus, either.

I yank off my donut apron and hop on the corduroy cushions and wrap myself in the army blanket. Before my papa even opens the book, my Gloaty Gus is circling round and round until he finds just the right spot, which of course is half on top of me. I sniff the warm smell of clumpy dog fur and the woodsy smell of Old Spice. My papa turns over an empty bucket of lemon filling and sits on top, his apron dragging on the floor. He clears his throat and opens the cover of *The World Book of Unbelievable and Spectacular Things*.

> *Did you know that you can't lick your own elbow?*
> *A coyote can hear a mouse under a foot of snow. True or false?*
> *The easiest way to catch a snake is with a forked stick that you make yourself.*

He holds up the page to show me the illustration of a Y-shaped branch.

It is the most delicious way to fall asleep, hearing my papa reading, his voice soft but deep, strong yet gentle. My eyes close as I snuggle deeper in the blanket and Augustus sighs. And that is the last thing I hear.

"What do you do when I am sleeping?" I ask my papa one day.

He chuckles. "Well, I make sure the coffeepot is ready for the morning. Then I carry you home."

I remember that. I remember the feeling of him rolling me tighter in the army blanket and then of him lifting me. My papa is a tall man, so I am not too big to carry, even last year when I was ten. I hear his key slide into the lock, hear the bolt snap in place, feel him pull the door to make sure the lock on the donut shop holds. And I remember the feeling of him walking home and of me swaying softly with each step. I have never been on a fishing boat, but I think being rocked on the waves must feel like this.

On that terrible night it is drizzling softly. One or two drops leave little wet prints on my nose. I tuck my face deeper in the blanket and smell the Old Spice and drift asleep to the rising and falling of the waves.

It all happens so fast, my papa groaning and slipping, and me landing on the sidewalk, and Augustus pushing on my nose as he checks if I am alive. I push him away and sit up and wipe the drizzle from my eyes. In the moonlight I can see my papa lying on his side. He is very still.

"Papa?"

29

My mum flies in from California wearing a gray suit and thin heels.

She smells like patchouli perfume, which I hate particularly. Her skin is pale as china and her hair is pulled back in a tight bun. Not a single curl bounces.

All I want is to hide under the army blanket and wrap myself around Augustus, but my mum says no, I have to go to school. Doctors tell her my papa could be in the hospital for a very long time—maybe he will never come home—and she sorts through his affairs and arranges everything and says after a few weeks that we have no choice but to sell the house, but who would want a donut shop? After hearing my mum complain all this time, Harry tells her to shut her trap. He will run it.

"But you have a job. That's ridiculous."

He scowls. "If I don't, we'll lose our shirts." Then he shoves his fishing hat onto his head and stomps off to say a few words to my papa, which will soon become a habit, morning and evening, every day, rain or shine. My grandpa retires from his job at the sandpits the next week.

A few days after that, on a day that turns out to be the second most horrible of my life, I walk in from school and our house has sold and my mum has given my Augustus away. All that is left is the sweet smell of clumpy dog fur on the couch.

"You did what?" I scream, looking behind the bookcase and in all the closets and under my bed. *"How could you?"*

Harry glares at my mum. "Why on earth did you do that, Deborah?"

"Because she can't bring a dog to California, that's why. I can't stay here forever and I'm too busy for a kid *and* a dog. I put an ad in the paper. Someone came and took it. That's all."

"But I love him!" I shriek, running through the house—from the living room to the kitchen and then up the steep steps to my bedroom with the peaked roof, over and over, believing that somehow, if I look hard enough, I will find my Gloaty Gus.

I dive into the pillow on the couch. I howl and my

heart breaks. Harry puts his hand on my shoulder. I feel his calluses through my T-shirt. "You know nothing about children, Deborah," my grandpa says in that rock-hard voice of his that makes even the rug straighten itself. Then he walks out and slams the door behind him.

"And you do?" she yells after him. She runs in the bathroom, turns on the shower, and sobs. Later I hear her on the phone: "I don't know what I'm going to *do*, Robert." Then she hangs up.

The next morning before I am out of bed, Harry is back and my mum is talking.

"I've changed my mind," she tells my grandpa. "I simply cannot bring a child to California."

"You're her mother, for God's sake, Deborah."

"I gave that up a long time ago, didn't I?" Her voice is taut, sharp, like fishing line.

Except for my mum's crying, there is silence. I hide under my army blanket and wait for my very bad dog Augustus to jump up and steal my fattest pillow—which of course he never does.

30

On the first night I live with Harry, he cooks creamed cod on toast for supper.

He eats cornflakes for breakfast, spoons mackerel out of a can for lunch.

He takes the long walk to see my papa at St. Camillus before he opens the donut shop, and again at night after he closes.

My headaches last all day.

The train clacks on its tracks and shakes me in my thin little bed, where I lie wrapped in my army blanket, desperately trying to trap the Old Spice smell, watching my window rattle, wondering if you can die from loneliness.

I believe that you can.

31

The only person more pig-stubborn than me is Harry.

This is why on the morning after I ride out to Swanson's and fly back to our skinny apartment without my dog, I look out my window and see the Blackbird sticking up out of the dumpster next to the Shop Value across the street.

The handlebars hang over the edge and a vegetable bag hooked to the metal basket flaps each time a truck roars by.

My belly twists. The floor tilts. I grab my bedpost.

Carp-face.

Then Cynthia is rushing across the road to have herself a look. She scrambles up the side of the dumpster and reaches in. My knuckles spark. I don't bother to brush my teeth.

There's a note on the kitchen table:

WORK FOR MRS. SALVATORE THIS MORNING.
MAKE SURE YOU ARE READY FOR YOUR TEACHER
AT THREE.

Pea-brained ox. I make up a trillion other cusswords about Harry as I race down our stairs and out onto the street so fast the milk truck swerves around me and I reach the dumpster just as Cynthia flicks the headlight on. Buzzards fly inside me.

"Look, it's your bike!" There's a happy-puppy sound in her voice.

Hornets whirl.

"I know *it's my bike*," I growl, making my voice as gruff as Harry's. "So get off."

While I scramble up the side, Cynthia pulls the Blackbird's front wheel and a terrible smell soars out of the dumpster. Flies dance fireworks over my head.

Cynthia gags. "There's something dead in there," she whimpers, backing off.

I ignore the scratching-little-feet sounds at the bottom of the dumpster. "Get out of here, Cynthia. This is my bike."

"But I saw your grandpa throw it away. I saw him march over here and dump it in. So it's mine, that's what my mama says—finders, keepers."

The idea of the Blackbird being ridden by someone like Cynthia makes my blood boil. I have no choice but to push her off the dumpster. When I do, she rolls and cries out, hugging her knees. "Why are you so mean all the time, Rosie?"

"I said leave my bike alone, Cynthia." I pull the handlebars, which makes the Blackbird's back wheel poke through a package of sausages. Someone tossed a few gallons of milk into the dumpster and there are bags of rotting lettuce and sacks of wet spinach and many jumbo packs of hamburger rolls. The flies circle and land. Maggots crawl across a package of chicken wings. Even my toes gag, and they are used to bad smells.

I yank on my bike and one of the pedals rips open a package of pork chops. I tug my shirt up over my nose. Cynthia retches.

We are interrupted by Swanson, who nearly hits us as she pulls into the parking lot. A moment later, she sideswipes Avery Taylor's red Camaro.

Cynthia stops gagging. The jeep jerks forward, scraping even more. The motor revs, then sits quiet. You can see Swanson through the window, pulling her hunting hat down over her bone face. A little boy walking beside a full grocery cart grabs his mother's hand.

I jump down from the dumpster because maybe my Gloaty Gus is in the jeep, but I see pretty quickly there is only Swanson. She grinds the motor and tries to pull out again, and there's more crunching until she finally stops and slumps into the seat.

Cynthia whimpers as Avery Taylor races out of the store, waving and screaming, his produce apron flapping behind him. She grabs my arm. Her chewed nails touch my skin. "She's going to cripple him in his sleep—she does that to people, you know."

"Where do you even come up with things like that?" I push her away from where she is trying to hide in my shirt.

"From my mama—she knows things."

I scoff. How can anyone even listen to a mother who doesn't make her kid brush her hair, and what about all the scratching? Harry won't even talk to Cynthia's mother when she brings him tuna noodle casseroles because of what she said after my papa went to St. Camillus, about how sometimes you don't recover from a stroke that bad. Harry believes in holding a grudge.

Folks pour out of the store, the bank, and Eddie's Barbershop across the street, then the police come and the grit blows down from the sandpits and we have a storm on our hands. An officer makes Swanson get out of her jeep. She tries to pull her wool hat lower.

While everyone is watching Swanson, I pull the Blackbird the rest of the way out of the dumpster and race it across Main Street. Its front wheel squeaks louder than Mrs. Salvatore's clothesline and the chain is hanging off.

I push my bike into the toolshed and run upstairs to take a bath.

I am surprised my grandpa is home.

God's bones.

32

Harry has stretched the phone wire into his bedroom, and the door is shut. He doesn't believe in cordless phones.

I tiptoe past just as his gravelly voice says, "If that's what you really want, Deborah. I'm too old to fight you anymore."

The earth tilts. I have to grab a chair.

Harry looks like he swallowed a camel when I barge in.

This time fire is falling from *my* fingers. He still has the phone in his hand.

Hornets whirl. "You want to get rid of me!"

"Where in the name of Pete did you come up with that?"

"I just *heard you talking*."

"Well, you shouldn't be sticking your nose where it doesn't belong." He slams the phone down.

I stamp my foot. "It is *my* business. And where's my bike, anyway?"

I wait for the guilty look to come in his eyes, but only a mad bull is sitting there. He doesn't explain himself. Instead, he sends me to work at Mrs. Salvatore's or else.

I am between a rock and a hard place. If I make Harry too mad, he will move me to California before I can get my dog.

"But take a bath first," my grandpa says. "You smell like a vulture."

Barf-beetle.

33

I take one look at Mrs. Salvatore's table with the mountain of peas that she wants me to shell, and believe me, I turn around and head out the way I came.

"You get back here, Rosalita, if you know what's good for you."

"It's *Rosie!*" My eyes pop.

"Didn't anyone ever teach you any manners, young lady?" She pulls a chair out for me.

Lions gnash my bones.

"I promised your grandfather a full report of how much work you do."

I think about that rock and that hard place and plop down beside Philippe, who is not shelling peas. He is drawing a map.

If my very bad dog Augustus was here, he'd jump on

the table and try and eat all the peas and I'd have to fill my voice with spikes and say a million *bad dog*s to make him stay on the floor and then he'd look at me with his gooseberry eyes and I'd get to feeling sorry about yelling at him awful bad and I'd scratch him between the ears the way he likes and give him half the peas.

My head pounds. I could use an ice cube.

Philippe's coat is buttoned to his chin, and his ears are very red. I'm going to need his help picking the padlock on Swanson's barn, and I consider the coat. My toes are doubtful. Can you even ride a bike in a coat that big?

"My mum's flying out," I tell him. "She wants to get involved in my future."

Philippe draws a wavy line for a river somewhere. "That sounds bad."

"Tell me about it."

I shell a few peas, then try and make my voice casual before I ask, "Do you have a bike?"

He shakes his head. I pick up a pea pod, slit it down the middle with my thumbnail, scrape four fat peas into my mouth, and try to come up with a plan.

Mrs. Salvatore carries a basket of towels into the kitchen, and I pause a moment between peas. "You know, Philippe's legs are skinny as straws. He needs a bike. It would help him build muscle."

I lift Philippe's coat so his legs stick out. "See?" He whips it back over his bony knees. Some people don't like to have their insides exposed, but I myself am used to it. Miss Holloway told so many people about my terrible year that I lost count. Even the lunch ladies know.

"We don't have any bikes here. You think I have money for luxuries like that, Rosalita Gillespie?" Mrs. Salvatore folds a big bath towel in seconds—first the two long edges, then flip flip flip. In less than a minute she has a pile a dozen towels high.

She doesn't answer me while she carries them into the bathroom, but when she comes back, she says, "You're right, though. I was just telling Philippe that he needs to stop playing Monopoly all the time and get his skinny self outside. See how pale he is?"

She pinches his cheek and leaves a red print. I point out that they sell bikes at the thrift store—and they are cheap.

Mrs. Salvatore notices how few peas I have shelled. "Jesus, Mary, and Joseph—you eat them all, Rosie, you'll be here till kingdom come."

She is interrupted by Paulie, who flies in the kitchen, wailing, "Francesca threw my turtle in the toilet, and now he's drowned."

We all rush into the bathroom and Mrs. Salvatore pulls a spotted turtle from the toilet.

"Is he drowned?" Paulie wails.

Mrs. Salvatore rubs the turtle's shell with her apron, looks deep into the space where its head is hiding, and after a moment puts it back into the little boy's hands. "He's fine."

The girl watches from the door and says in a muffled voice, "He just wanted to swim."

"Ralph doesn't need to swim, Francesca. Ralph isn't a pond turtle, he's a *house turtle*." Francesca covers her face with her hands and begins to sob. Mrs. Salvatore pulls her close. "Oh my goodness, what did I ever do to God to get so many naughty children?"

If I wasn't in such a hurry to get Philippe to the thrift store to look for a bike, I might point out that maybe she shouldn't take in every child who knocks on her door. We watch Paulie whisper softly to the turtle. Then Mrs. Salvatore goes to the kitchen and dumps another bag of peas on the table.

"Rosie, after you finish these peas, maybe—just maybe—I'll let you take Philippe to the thrift store and see what they have for bikes."

"But this will take forever." I let a little whine fall out of my mouth.

"All right, then, no bike."

I am frustrated like I used to be when my papa took me to church and the listening part took forever and I swung my legs back and forth and thumped the pew in front of me. "Stop being a bear," he would say.

I take a deep breath. "I really hate shelling peas, Mrs. Salvatore."

She looks from me to the pile on the table—so high there must be a million in there—and snorts. Then she reaches in an old salt container and pulls out twenty dollars. "What did I ever do to get a girl like you, Rosie? Now hurry, before I change my mind."

34

The bike outside the Church of Our Risen Lord thrift shop is red and shines brighter than the Blackbird ever did. I count twelve gears.

Philippe stands back, but I run my hands all over the glistening paint and test the brakes (they work) and switch the gears (they click like they get oiled *with love* twice a day). I push on the seat (no squeaking) and check the price tag.

I hoped Philippe would find a bike that looked like mine. I look around for a worse bike, but this is the only one.

It's not fair that this weird boy could get a bike with brakes that work with just a touch of his hands, while I have to drag my feet for miles just to start slowing down. I breathe many times to get the bitter taste out of my mouth.

"Why would someone want to get rid of this bike?" I ask, walking around and around. "There's got to be something wrong with it."

I look the frame over, though, and it is solid and straight. The bike has a racing seat and black handgrips. The kickstand is solid as a fence post.

"Well, what do you think?"

Philippe shrugs and rolls his eyes.

"If you're going to ride a bike this good, you should at least be a little excited about it." I scoot down and examine the way the front wheel sits arrow-straight. This bike is good enough to go under a Christmas tree.

I am green.

I decide I better see how it rides. I climb on without asking and pedal out through the parking lot and onto Main Street, feeling the perfect ease of the gears, the lovely way it spins and turns, hearing the gravel spit and spray under the tires.

When I get back, Philippe has filled his pockets with cans. I get off the bike and hand it to him. "Try it."

He slips a little further into his coat. He doesn't take the bike. "Well?" I say, pushing it to him. "You should at least act a teeny bit grateful. Otherwise, you don't deserve it."

Philippe watches me for a moment, then takes the handlebars and climbs on. His lumpy coat gets caught on the seat; a can falls out of his pocket.

"You can't wear that when you ride," I snap.

He looks at the ground. Then he climbs off, hands the bike to me, and heads for home.

I run after him, catch his coat, whip him around.

"What is the matter with you? I really need you to help me get my dog. Swanson locked him in her barn and I need you to help me pick the lock. *You need to ride this bike.*"

Philippe scowls. "I don't like to ride bikes."

"How can you not like to ride bikes? *Everybody* likes riding bikes."

He shrugs, picks up another can, stuffs it into his pocket. "No one ever taught me how."

I march back into the Church of Our Risen Lord thrift store, buy the bike, and fly it home.

Hornets whirl.

35

The sidewalk flinches as flames fall off Harry's feet.

"I'm paying good money for this teacher and I told you *three o'clock.*"

"You don't have to drag me."

My toes wince from walking so fast. "What does it matter if I see this teacher when *you're going to make me go live with my mum* anyway?" Sheet metal wraps around my heart and I clamp my teeth.

Harry grunts and lets the door of the donut shop slam in my face.

Mr. Peterson is already squeezed into the last booth. One of his little girls speeds a fire truck through a hill of sugar on the floor, a boy crawls over the teacher's Santa belly and sticks a straw in his beard, and the twins are writing in notebooks that look just like the one he gave me.

Rainbow sprinkles and broken donut pieces and strawberry jelly are smeared onto the table, and the girl on the floor is pouring out more sugar.

Mr. Peterson ignores the noise as his hand flies across the page of a notebook in front of him.

Harry marches me toward the booth. "Clean it up," he tells the little girl on the floor. She jumps up quickly because of the steel in his voice and drops the sugar pourer. It rolls until it hits one of the stools at the counter.

"Apologize!" he roars at me, then clomps into the back room so he won't have to talk to anyone else.

Mr. Peterson clears a spot on the table and pushes a plate of gooey brownies toward me. "My wife made these for you."

I like brownies very much, so I wipe a spot of donut jelly off the seat and sit. I push a brownie into my mouth and notice the children watching me. Mr. Peterson jiggles the table a little so there is more room for his son to crawl over his belly. The girl brings the sugar pourer back.

"I'm just finishing up my story for you." He pats the notebook in front of him.

My teeth ring from all the sugar in the chocolate. I reach for another brownie. Mr. Peterson sips his tea.

"I'm very interested in how your story is coming along. Did you bring the notebook?"

I wince over how the chocolate makes my teeth ache and don't answer him. I push my finger in figure eights through the jelly on the table.

"I see," he says finally. He eats one of my brownies, and chocolate crumbs settle into his beard.

"I checked your test scores—before last year they were off the charts." He pulls the little boy away from the plate of brownies. "Now, you and I both know that you should be in my class." He watches me but I am careful to keep going with my figure eights.

"But in order to get into my class—where I'm sure you've heard we shoot for the moon—you're going to have to prove you've got some life in that brain of yours. You're going to have to write your story."

I roll my eyes and eat another brownie. If my very bad dog Augustus was here, he would watch me with his gooseberry eyes, and just having him adoring all over me like that would quiet the leopards gnashing deep inside my ears. He always knew what I was feeling about everything.

I check to make sure Harry isn't watching me make figure eights. "Can't you give me worksheets or something?"

The teacher tents his fingers and looks at me through the space he's made. "You know how to write boring stuff, I bet, like what's the best trip you ever took or about your best friend, or any number of silly prompts I could give you, but do you know what it feels like to be writing from way down deep inside, where you're writing so fast you feel like a train flying down the tracks and you don't know where you're going and you don't care, all you want is to go on and on?"

I eat another brownie and make my belly as big as a barrel.

He rips a page from his notebook and pushes it across the table. "I've started writing my story. I want you to have it."

I check to see if Harry is watching. Mr. Peterson's handwriting is so messy it feels like I'm finding my way through the dark.

36

Rosie, when I was your age, I threw up every time I got nervous—and I was a very nervous kid.

I threw up at swimming lessons, in gym class, and on the playground. Soon I was nervous about getting nervous. And then I was nervous about getting nervous about being nervous. You get the idea.

I was nervous about riding the bus and throwing up on the bus, I was nervous about taking tests and throwing up on my desk, I was nervous about reading out loud, I was nervous about my classmates laughing at my mother's egg salad sandwiches.

I was very skinny, a terrible runner, I couldn't swim, I fell off my bike constantly, and I couldn't catch a ball. I threw up on the sand at swimming lessons because I was afraid of the water, and I threw up on my sleeping bag at Cub Scout camp because I was afraid of the woods.

My mother said I had a nervous stomach and would outgrow it. Eventually she gave up and kept me home.

This is the truth, it is something that happened to me, and it shaped me. It gave me gifts that I have used throughout my life. What gifts, you might ask, would someone get from throwing up all the time? It made me strong. Heck, if I could get through that, I could get through anything.

It made me unsinkable. Absolutely unsinkable.

The little boy sticks a spoon in his father's beard. Mr. Peterson grabs it and slides the boy out of the way. I push the page back. I stare at the teacher so long my eyes cramp.

"I'm never going to do this," I whisper.

"Your choice. I won't ask for the transfer and you can go to the other class."

I crack my knuckles as Mr. Peterson piles up his things. "Let me know if you write anything." He leads his children out of the donut shop and leaves the page on the table.

I eat the rest of the brownies and stare at the page until the letters swarm. Then I stuff it in my pocket, walk home, and go straight to my bed, where I practice being a whale.

When the phone rings, I let it go until it stops.

37

Word gets around that I am trying to teach Philippe to ride a bike and right away we get an audience.

Cynthia walks out first, a Barbie in each hand. "Wow, that's a nice bike. Where'd you get that?"

"Go away," I snap.

She tries to touch the handlebars. "I used to have a bike, but it was one with training wheels, and I'm really good at bike riding now, so can I have a turn?"

I get so distracted that I push Philippe right over my toe. "No, *you cannot have a turn!*" I roar. "You can just go home. We don't need anyone watching—he's terrible enough as it is."

Well, this is the wrong thing to say because Cynthia wails and I can't hear myself think and then Philippe climbs off, drops the bike on the ground, and storms off.

"I'm sorry, I'm sorry, I'm sorry," I cry, rushing after him, grabbing his coat. "I didn't mean to say that. It's just that I miss my dog so much and I need you to help me get him back and the only way you can help me is if you learn to ride a bike. It's too far to walk and Harry would never bring me."

Philippe scowls. Sweat drips down my neck. I push my springy curls behind my ears. "If you ever had a dog, you'd know how important this is."

"Shut up, Rosie. You act like you're the only one who ever lost a dog. But you're not."

His eyes spark and he unbuttons his top button.

"I know *that*. Did I ever say I am the only one who ever lost a dog?"

"You sure act like it."

To tell you the truth, it does feel like I am the only one sometimes. I don't tell him that. I take a loud wet breath. I watch Cynthia wipe her eyes on her sleeve. I turn back to the boy in the gigantic coat. "Are you going to help me or not?"

I hold out the bike.

"Where's his helmet?" Mrs. Salvatore yells, flying out from our apartment building, her apron flapping, all the little foster children scurrying behind her. Of course, everyone wants a turn.

My God, this is going to take me forever. Pretty soon, Eddie the Barber walks out because it is lunch break, and the milkman (on his lunch break, too) comes over and says, "Well, he's got to take that coat off. You can't ride with your coat dragging like that."

Philippe locks down, stiffens, and clenches his jaw. "Go away," I tell everyone.

Believe me, I try all the tricks my papa taught me, including the one that worked for me: go up a very small grassy hill and, pedaling constantly, fly down. The hill will help you learn to balance; the grass will keep you from going too fast and it will cushion you if you fall.

But Philippe wobbles and bobs until his perfectly straight front wheel shakes and he topples over.

I am so thirsty I could drink a pond. I am irritated because everyone has advice. Plus, there's a breeze blowing and grit is flying up my nose.

38

When Harry climbs the hill, he brings a wrench. The first thing he says is "Take that coat off."

Philippe tightens his grip on the handlebars and watches his feet, but Harry has concrete running down his back.

Finally, after about ten thousand years, Philippe sighs and takes the coat off and drops it on the ground. I have never seen him without it and I am surprised how his neck looks a little chickenlike because it is so long and thin. Also, his chest is slender as a fish and the pointy bones in his shoulders pop up. He doesn't have enough fat on him to float.

Philippe shivers without the coat, even as the sun blazes.

Harry clears his throat a few times, then turns to me

and slaps the wrench in my hands. "Now take the pedals off."

"What?" I am incredulous.

We'll never get out to Swanson's farm without pedals.

Harry whips the wrench out of my hands, kneels, and groans as his knees hit the grit. "Quickest way to learn to ride a bike. We used to do it to soldiers who couldn't ride."

Once both pedals are lying on the ground, Harry lowers the seat as far as it will go. He holds the bike up. "Try this," he tells Philippe. "Keep pushing yourself along with your feet. And you should be on flat ground. Hills are for when you got some balance."

He glares at me.

"Pedals worked just fine for me," I snort, my voice blade-sharp.

Harry brushes his knees. "Well, thank God the world isn't made up entirely of Rosie Gillespies."

He turns to Philippe and says, "You do it my way and you'll be riding in about ten minutes. And keep the coat off."

Well, Harry is right and it doesn't take long for Philippe to get the hang of it. He is zooming across the yard and down the hill behind the apartments, and he doesn't wobble at all. It's like he has natural balance, and his bike sparkles in the sun. I try and get rid of the bitter feeling in my heart.

Cynthia claps. I hold my breath. Mrs. Salvatore yells, "Careful, not too fast!" and other things like that.

By suppertime we put the pedals back on. Philippe rides down the hill and doesn't fall off. I notice a sour taste in my belly.

"Tomorrow we go get my dog," I snap as we drag the bike up to Philippe's apartment.

"You're going to just take him? Isn't that stealing?"

I blow my breath out in a loud, furious whoosh.

"It's not stealing when it's your dog."

39

On Tuesday afternoons Harry whistles.

This is because he closes the donut shop early so he can play blackjack at the American Legion. This makes him happy.

I don't have to cook, because Harry brings pizza home. This makes me happy, even if I do have to pick all the anchovies off.

A fly buzzes against the window screen. I take the biggest bite of pizza I can and turn *Jeopardy!* on. Harry snaps it off and drops his book on vexillology beside the pizza box. The table slumps under the weight.

"If you just put a little effort in, you would enjoy this." He pushes the book to me, takes a slice of pizza from the box, piles on all the anchovies I pulled off. He wipes his mouth with the back of his hand.

The book is thick as a tomb. Even my chair rolls its eyes.

"Well?" Harry thumps the book.

I open the first page and try to focus because there will be a quiz later. *"Vexillology is the study of flags, taken from the Latin word* vexillum. *The term was used in ancient times to describe cloth suspended from a pole."*

I am bored in three seconds. The cat clock above the sink sweeps its black tail back and forth, *ticktock*. A hot breeze snaps through the screens and I have to cover my slice of pizza from the grit.

Harry traveled the world when he was a marine and someday—"God only knows when that will be now"—he's going to buy a camper and collect a flag from every state. I think he should spend some of that travel money on air-conditioning. I lift the springy curls off the back of my neck. My blood begins a slow boil.

I look at the clock, tap my feet. Finally, my plan is in place. My brain keeps zigzagging around the idea that Swanson has had my Augustus this whole time. My toes are impatient to get going: *tap-tap-tap*.

"Stop that." Harry's brow darkens.

I put one foot on top of the other to stop the tapping. Then my fingers take off across the tabletop: *tap-tap-tap*.

I go back to the book. *"Long ago, knights carried flags*

into battle because it was hard to tell who the enemy was when everyone was suited up in armor."

Hornets whirl. How many hours before it will be too dark to ride? Can Philippe even ride his bike in the dark?

"Well?" Harry watches my hands *tap-tap-tap*. He glances out the window. He looks down at my feet, *thump-thump-thump*. He narrows his eyes. "Don't even think about going anywhere tonight. I want you here doing the work for that teacher."

My throat knots. Harry still hasn't figured out I rescued my bike from the dumpster. I pretend to be interested in the book and make my fingers behave. I glance at the clock, feel all shivery from the sweat dripping down my back. My toes tap again and I push them against the floor until they squeal.

Harry snorts, gets up, and comes back with two dozen little flags on wooden pedestals. He sets them on the table, counting under his breath, trying to get control of his temper. There's starch in his voice when he says, "I'm bringing some up to your father."

I scowl. My papa doesn't need flags. He used to tell everybody at the donut shop that when he got sick with the flu, you could just forget about doctors because the only things that fixed him up were a cup of Campbell's chicken noodle soup (made by me), a book (read out loud by me), and my dog (snuggled up beside us with that Gloaty Gus grin on him and his tail thumping a mile a minute).

I snort.

That's enough for Harry. He picks up his little flags and shoves them into a paper bag. He throws the pizza box into the trash and checks if I put any more cans in there.

He sees my fingers tapping again. He raises an eyebrow, watches my thumb drum the table. He narrows his eyes. "You better be here all night writing in that notebook."

I check the clock. Fire ants march behind my eyes.

When Harry finally grabs his fishing hat and walks up the road with the sack of flags, the phone rings again. I bet a billion dollars it is my mum, because who else ever calls?

I let it ring ten times before it stops.

Harry doesn't believe in answering machines.

On this, we agree.

40

The Blackbird squeaks all the way up Swanson's hill. I blow my breath out in a loud huff as Philippe pedals his shiny red bike up the steep slope. The belt buckle from his wool coat drags in the grit behind him.

"Oh, come on," I howl, "you'd be faster if you got off and pushed."

Already it is late afternoon. Harry has been playing cards for an hour. I had to promise Philippe that I would play a thousand games of Monopoly (a promise I don't intend to keep) before he'd come.

Mrs. Salvatore is serving shepherd's pie at the Church of Our Risen Lord supper, and she brought all the other kids with her. I told her I would help Philippe practice on his bike if he didn't have to go and that we would be back before dark.

"You promise he will wear his helmet?"

"Yes," I said as casually as I could, trying to keep the hurry out of my voice.

When Philippe finally reaches me, his chest heaves and underneath his helmet his pale curls stick to his face. He has raccoon eyes from the marks left by the new pair of swimming goggles Harry bought him at Walmart.

"Why do you wear that stupid coat? Anyone with any sense at all would know it's too hot." I push my water bottle in his hand or else we'll never make it to Swanson's.

Philippe flops in the gully, gulping. I scrape the heel of my sneaker so hard in the grit on the road that sparks fly.

A crow soars to the top of Swanson's barn and swallows dive from the hayloft and plunge over the field toward the apple trees and the chicken coop beyond. A rusted tractor sits in the field, strung up with poison ivy. The driveway is empty—Swanson isn't home.

Philippe gulps more water, tipping the bottle straight up so everything drains out, leaving nothing for the ride home.

"Well, that was stupid." I count to a million, glaring at him. "Hurry up."

He wheezes. "I don't know about this, Rosie. Cynthia says Swanson shoots squirrels."

Sharks swarm my eyes. "All the more reason to get my dog out of there, *wouldn't you say?*"

41

I wait for Philippe to catch up at the barn. His chest heaves under his coat. I frown and hold out my hand with the paper clips.

He just stares. "I can't use these on a lock this big. This lock's way bigger than the one on the shed."

I blink.

"You need a metal tool, like a file."

I breathe in sharply. "Well, why didn't you bring the right tools? You're the one who's the expert, so *you should have brought the right ones.*"

He takes one of the paper clips from my hand and bends it like limp spaghetti. "See?"

A hawk screams in the distance. Rats gnaw inside my head and I would like to kick Philippe.

I look around wildly, wondering what to do next.

There's the narrow window on the side of the barn, but we don't have a ladder. I pull him over.

Philippe considers it for only a second before he whispers, "Are you crazy? How will we get up there?"

Sometimes it's better when he doesn't talk. "You can give me a boost. Now hold out your hands."

Philippe doesn't take his hands out of his pockets.

"Haven't you ever given anyone a boost before? You lace up your fingers like this." I show him. When he fixes his hands, I step up and reach for the window, but he wobbles right away. "Aw, Rosie, you're too heavy."

In my whole life no one has ever said I was too heavy. This is infuriating, I can tell you that. "Just keep still," I hiss.

"We don't have to do this," he says, trying to make his voice tough as I pull myself up. "You can just tell your grandfather that your dog is here and he'll come and help."

"Don't you think I've already thought of that? Harry says our apartment is too small for a dog. If you had a dog as wonderful as Augustus, you would do this, too. Friends do things for each other. Now stay still." I grab on to the window frame and inch my way higher.

"Ouch!" he yelps.

"Philippe, you have to stand still!"

When I finally get my head up to the window, I have

a good view of the inside. There is an old tractor, a lawn mower wedged against the wall, some saws, a wheel-barrow, paint buckets, steps leading to a hayloft, and no dog. My heart sinks as I try to push the window up, but Philippe wobbles and his legs sway and I grab on to the ledge. "What are you doing? You're going to drop me!"

"You weigh a ton, Rosie."

"I do not weigh a ton. I weigh less than you. Now hold me up."

Philippe grunts and boosts me up and I squint, searching further into the barn. I stretch my head a bit higher so I can see what's that door at the very back, just a little more, just a bit, then a little more—and that's when I see a giant bag of dog food leaning near the hayloft. I sing a little hallelujah, I can tell you that.

I push the window and it creaks up about three inches and then jams. I wiggle it, but it won't budge.

"Rosie, there's no way you're going to get a dog out that window—even if you can get it open. And I don't hear a dog anyway."

"Stop talking like that, Philippe. You promised me if I keep playing Monopoly—and let you be the dog—that you'd help."

"Yeah, but you haven't played yet, have you?" He glares up at me, his eyes glinting the color of the sky.

"Oh, be quiet. There's a room way in the back. I

can see it. Augustus must be in there, sleeping or something." I decide not to tell Philippe my dog sleeps like a bear. I use the strength of my shoulder to push the window frame, then wiggle the sash. With another push, it inches up.

"See?" I snap, making my voice sound all know-it-all, trying to ignore my toes, which are warning me, *Even a bear would wake up by now.*

I look further inside, squinting, forcing my eyes to search all the way to the very back of the barn. Philippe tries to boost me higher and sways. His hands shake, but I stretch my head a bit higher so I can see what's back there, just a little more, just a bit—and then Philippe's legs buckle and his fingers unlace and I hurtle to the ground, jamming my knee. I roll around, holding my leg and groaning, while everything goes numb.

"Are you hurt?" he whispers.

"Of course I'm hurt, you idiot." Hornets whirl.

Somehow, while I am rolling around, we hear Swanson's jeep pull into the driveway.

"She's going to find us!" Philippe cries, and I stop rolling so I can pay attention. "Rosie, we've got to get out of here."

We both notice the lump the size of a turnip rising on my knee. My eyes fill and I angrily swipe them dry. "You promised you would help me get my dog, Philippe.

And who says she's coming out here? She's probably just going in her house."

"You're crazy," he says, sinking into his coat, stepping backward toward the woods.

"I am not. When you make a promise to help someone get her dog, you have to keep it. That's just the way it is. And besides, you dropped me, so you owe me."

"You fell!" He glares at me.

"I've loved my dog my whole life, Philippe."

He hesitates. He wipes his curls off his forehead and looks up at the narrow window. "But how do you know your dog is even in there?"

"We won't know until we go see!" My knee throbs.

"Well," he says after a minute, "I'm not boosting someone as heavy as you up there again, so I'm finding a log. Wait here."

I snort, steam flying out both ears. I check to see if the bone is sticking out. (It's not.) Then I stagger to my feet. I breathe deeply to keep from passing out from the pain and hold on to the side of the barn.

42

Philippe disappears into the woods. His coat camouflages him in the thick shade. A few minutes later, when he finally drags an old stump to the barn, his face is very red.

"That will never work," I snap. "Can't you see it's not tall enough?"

"It's all there was. You just have to pull yourself a little. Step up on this stump, hold on to the window, and pull."

"With my knee I'm supposed to do that?" I try to catch the whine that falls out of my mouth.

We both look at the cuts and at the lump getting even bigger. "Rosie, I already told you I don't want to do this. What if there are snakes?"

"Snakes don't live in barns," I scoff. "They live in basements."

"Well, what if there are holes in the floor?"

"Philippe, just do it. If you ever had a friend before, you'd know friends help each other."

He rolls his eyes, then climbs up the stump, grabs hold of the top of the window frame, swings a second, and jumps inside. When I follow him and look in, he is holding his arms out to catch me, and I am grateful for the thick wool coat. His curls are stuck to his cheeks, and for a moment, because he is helping me get my dog, I love that face. I ignore my toes, which keep warning me about how my dog isn't barking, then arrows shoot up my leg and I remember how mad I am at everything and I jump like a stormtrooper—only it's a little too much, a little too far, and I fly further than I wanted to and flip right past Philippe's open arms and onto the floor. I see stars.

I wince, rolling around and moaning. I knock a paint bucket over and it clatters along the floor.

"Your dog isn't even here," Philippe snaps. "If he was, he would be barking."

Hornets whirl.

43

Somehow, over the clamor, we hear footsteps on the gravel outside. Philippe grabs my shirt and tugs so hard the neck rips. "We have to go!"

I hold my breath and listen. My knee throbs. The stones crunch outside. Swanson is very close.

"We have to go—now!" Philippe whispers fiercely, stepping toward the window, but I grab his coat.

"We can't *leave*, Philippe. I'm not going without my dog."

"But she's coming. And your dog isn't *even here*."

"Well then, he must be in the house. I'm not leaving without him." I point to the hayloft. "You have to help me up there." I pull his arm.

Swanson fiddles with the padlock. Then a dog yelps from outside. My toes warn me that it doesn't sound like Augustus at all.

"Oh boy," Philippe whispers.

We hear more dog yapping as Swanson fiddles with the lock and I hobble as fast as I can up the hayloft ladder and when Swanson pushes the doors open I am just pulling hay over our heads and we are alone in the dark underneath. I hold my knee.

The dog pants, moans, whines. Philippe stiffens. Trying not to breathe, wanting to sneeze, we listen as Swanson and the dog walk slowly through the barn. I imagine her shoes flapping off her heels like when she was a girl at school with my papa.

The bales are heavy; the hay scratches. I get very thirsty very quickly and try to think of something other than my aching knee. I bury my face in Philippe's coat, grateful for its woolly lumpiness. His chest beats like there is a bird trapped in there.

The dog whines. Swanson walks toward the back of the barn, then the paint can clatters against the wall. I reach for Philippe's hand.

Philippe doesn't move. My ears tense, listening, straining so hard I could hear grass grow.

44

Swanson whistles softly.

We hear dog nails click quickly toward us, and then Swanson's footsteps start slowly up the ladder.

I hold my breath. Seconds last centuries. Blood pounds in my head. Philippe shudders and squirms. I have to pinch his arm to keep him still.

Swanson steps onto the loft. The dog growls. Swanson makes an odd clucking noise and it quiets. I am close to passing out. The dry smell of the hay scratches against the back of my throat and I need to cough. Philippe sinks against my chest. I say a silent prayer that his coat isn't sticking out.

The boards creak as Swanson walks closer. She moves some of the hay bales in front of us and Philippe makes a little moan. I take a teeny breath, then bury the air deep in my lungs and keep it there. Swanson pushes a few more bales. She is only the length of the donut case away. Philippe slumps deeper into his coat and I try to hold him steady. Finally, when I am so dizzy and faint that the dark under the hay begins to glint and pop like a Fourth of July sparkler, Swanson gives up, piles the bales back into place, and climbs down the ladder. She makes that clucking noise and the dog follows her out of the barn, growling every few steps. We hear Swanson snap the padlock into place.

In the muffled silence under the hay, I touch Philippe's face and put my arm around him. I know that wasn't my dog. My Augustus would have never left without me.

"Come on," I say, making Philippe drag an old oil barrel to the window so we can both climb out—me with my shrieking knee.

"I can't just leave my dog here," I say when we get outside.

"Well, I'm not staying another minute. They're all going to get home from that church supper soon."

I stomp my good foot.

"I'm not leaving without my dog."

"That dog didn't sound like the big bear-dog you're always talking about. It sounded smaller. I bet it wasn't even your dog."

I am incensed. "I know it wasn't my dog. My dog must be in the house. I know I heard *my dog* when I was here before." Vipers hiss behind my ears.

Philippe waits a couple of seconds for me to follow him, and when I don't, he flies off for the woods, the belt from his coat clacking behind him.

I hobble a few feet into the shade and wait for him to come back and apologize.

After about a hundred years, when he doesn't return, I give up and limp toward my bike. The chain is hanging off and I have to use a stick to poke it back on because I forgot to bring Harry's wrench.

As I get it clicked into place, a screeching motor flies up over the hill and sends a cloud of grit up my nose. I yank my bike into the bushes as Avery Taylor's red Camaro hurtles by. The top is down and the music blares. His friends are hollering in the backseat, waving their hockey sticks.

I flatten myself against the prickers as Avery Taylor skids to a stop in front of Swanson's, climbs out, and runs up the driveway with a paint bucket swinging from his hands. When he dumps paint all over her black jeep, sunflower-yellow splotches drip onto the driveway.

That's really terrible, my papa sighs in my head.

*　*　*

By the time I get home, I've had plenty of time to plan out how I'm going to make Philippe pay for leaving me behind.

My knee is swollen and will barely bend. I hunt through Harry's medicine cabinet and find a nearly empty bottle of Mercurochrome tincture "for cuts and wounds."

Half the label is worn off. I open the top and smell it. It looks like cherry Kool-Aid and I use the eyedropper to spread some on my cuts.

It burns like fire ants and I yell even louder than Mrs. Salvatore, which is saying a lot, I can tell you that.

45

You would think I committed murder, the way Mrs. Salvatore acts when she gets a whiff of how I never did get around to warning Philippe about Gorilla Dog.

I am sitting in the tub the next morning soaking my knee, trying to come up with a new plan, when a roaring bull bangs at our door. "Rosalita, I know you're in there! What in God's name did I ever do to deserve this?"

Her eyes spit when I finally open the door. "I should take a switch to you. How could you leave him there like that, Rosalita?"

I step back, pull the thin towel around me tighter. "What are you talking about?"

"That dog, that terrible dog. It chewed Philippe like a little meatball. You let him ride ahead like that,

Rosalita, the first time he ever rode his bike so far, and you didn't even tell him to be careful?"

That's when I snap. "Do you know what he did?" I yell right back at her. "I was hurt *really bad* and my chain kept falling off and I had to coast my bike most of the way home and he rushed off and left *me!*"

I lift the towel so she can see my knee.

Mrs. Salvatore hardly looks at it. Instead, she tells me that's it, get dressed, follow her. I have to watch Paulie, Francesca, and the baby because she is taking Philippe to the doctor for a tetanus shot and Sarah is at the library.

"God knows that boy has had enough," she says, waiting until I get dressed, then marching me back to her apartment. "You don't even know what he's been through, do you, Rosalita?"

I am so sizzling mad at Philippe I couldn't care less. Mrs. Salvatore takes my arm and leads me into her apartment.

46

Philippe sits on the kitchen counter, holding a bag of frozen peas on his leg. He is wearing his heavy wool coat.

"That coat probably saved his neck," Mrs. Salvatore says, then gives Francesca and Paulie instructions on how to behave when she is gone.

She turns to me. "The lunch is peanut butter sandwiches, and don't forget that Paulie likes his peanut butter on the bottom and jelly on the top. And it has to be grape jelly, and don't mix it up. Remember: peanut butter on the bottom, jelly on the top. Plus, the laundry has to come in off the line before it rains, and fold everything right away—otherwise, I'll have to iron it all. And heaven forbid, don't I have enough to do without having to iron, too?"

Paulie comes up and tries to lift the peas off Philippe's leg. Philippe scowls and pushes him away.

"Mama!" screams Paulie, but Mrs. Salvatore is already saying, "Don't you *mama* me, Paulie, and don't you fight with Francesca while I'm gone."

Even I know this is just an invitation for him to go in the other room and clobber her. But before I say that, Mrs. Salvatore gives Philippe a little squeeze and whispers, "What in God's name did I ever do to get a boy as wonderful as you?" Then she helps him off the counter and he limps quite a bit as he walks to the door.

"When we are done with the doctor," Mrs. Salvatore says, "we are stopping at the police station and I am giving them a piece of my mind. Why folks in this town have put up with that dog for so long is beyond me."

She stops, eyes me carefully.

"And tomorrow you are coming with us. It's time you saw why we are so lucky to have Philippe in our lives."

I stare at her, my mouth open all the way to Africa.

Shoot me, please.

47

The next morning Mrs. Salvatore takes Philippe's arm and they walk up the long set of stone steps to the Church of Our Risen Lord.

Philippe's belt buckle clacks on the steps behind them. I stay where I am.

I do not like churches and I do not like what goes on inside them. I especially do not like all the talk about do-gooding, as Harry calls it—and all the pitying looks from church ladies wondering how I am getting on.

I dislike mostly everything about this place, including the incense that scratches my nose.

"I'll wait here." I say it firm and look Mrs. Salvatore in the eye when she turns around. I am serious about this.

"No, Rosalita. We are all going inside, and that means you. It's time you saw what life is about."

"Well, I'm not going to find out in there," I snap.

"Ha ha, you think you're so smart, but you're too big for your britches, that's what you are. Now follow me."

She reaches for my arm, but I push my hands into the very bottom of my pockets and twist until threads pop. Philippe limps up the steps, hidden in his coat, looking like a stuffed sausage, and when he stumbles, I grab his elbow.

I see how I am going to have to talk to him about a few more things if he is going to make it in this world— like how to watch where you are going.

"Rosie, I mean *now*. Or do you want me to tell your grandfather you let that awful dog attack Philippe?"

I fume. "I didn't *let* him get attacked. Philippe left me with a broken bike. Why doesn't anyone ever remember that?"

"No back talk," she says, holding the heavy door open. "I've had it up to here. And I mean it. We will march straight for the donut shop if you don't follow me this very instant."

I twist my fists deeper in my pockets, bristling, and finally, seeing no other option, follow this weird boy in the gigantic coat up the steps.

Mrs. Salvatore leads us through the heavy wooden doors and kneels, crosses herself, and moves into a back pew. She turns around and watches to make sure we are doing the same, which Philippe does. I am not one for kneeling or crossing myself, and neither is Harry, and so I humph and just sit down.

I swing my legs and look around. It has been ages since I've been here and it takes a few minutes to get my eyes right. I've never been here during the week—only on Sundays. The first interesting thing I notice is the church is unlocked. Why do they do that—wouldn't somebody steal stuff? Also, there's an oil lamp with a flame flickering up front— what about fire? The third thing—and I notice this after a few minutes of sitting here—is how peaceful you can get inside yourself when you breathe in all this quiet. It is a good place to think about things.

I accidentally thump the pew in front of me. Mrs. Salvatore gives me a look.

Philippe hunches further down in his coat. I wonder what he is thinking about and why we are even here. Then Mrs. Salvatore sighs a very big sigh, the kind I have noticed sometimes when I am over peeling potatoes or husking corn and it is the end of a very long day and all her laundry is done and the supper dishes are washed and the stove is shined and the floor is mopped for the last time of the day and she flops on the couch and puts her feet up on the coffee table. Her terry slippers have holes all over. It is that kind of sigh.

48

To tell you the truth, I get so lost in thinking up a new plan for getting my dog that I lose track of time. Mrs. Salvatore has to poke me.

Then she leads us down the stairs to the church basement, where there is a very simple room with a couch and two chairs, a coffee table, and a cross on the wall. There are donuts on the table.

"Good morning, Philippe." A woman in a black trench coat hurries over. Her voice has that singsong tone that grown-ups use when they try too hard. Harry never talks like this and neither does Mrs. Salvatore, but Miss Holloway uses it on her favorites. I roll my eyes.

Philippe pushes his face down so far into his coat that only his eyes show. The woman holds out her hand for Philippe. He watches his sneakers instead. This reminds me I need to have a talk with him about shaking with a firm grip.

Then she tells Mrs. Salvatore it's highly unusual for a visitor (meaning me) to be present at a meeting, but maybe if we don't make a big deal out of it, all will go okay.

Just as I'm trying to figure out who she is, the real reason we are here comes clomping out of the bathroom. A lady with wide cheeks and snipped pale hair rushes toward Philippe, her arms open wide. "I was in the john so long I almost missed all the fun, now didn't I, Philippe, my baby boy?" Her laugh is scratchy—a smoker. "Now come, Philippe, come give your big ole mama a hug."

Philippe's mama?

Philippe dips lower into his coat and tries to sink through the floor. The lady wears a flowered blouse with buttons missing and a jelly roll of fat pops out. She holds her arms wide. My jaw unhinges from hanging open so long. Philippe stands where he is, buried inside his coat.

"What's the matter with him, he won't come and hug his own mama?" she says, turning to the other woman, who I now realize must be the social worker. Then Philippe's mama turns to Mrs. Salvatore. "You did this, didn't you? You told him things about me, made him this way. I just want to give my baby boy some love." There's a little whimper in her voice and she holds her arms out again. Someone should tell this woman to stop calling Philippe a baby boy.

"And who are you?" she says, noticing me. "I don't let my boy have girlfriends." She turns to the social worker. "Get her out of here."

Girlfriend?

I can hardly believe my ears. If my mouth wasn't closing up on me, I'd tell her a thing or two—like *I don't even hardly like your son.* I glare at her.

"Now, now, Mrs. Brown," the social worker says, putting her arm on the woman's shoulder. "You remember what we talked about."

"Don't tell me what we talked about. I expect my son to give me a hug when he hasn't seen me in a month." She takes a step toward Philippe.

"Mrs. Brown, get control of yourself."

But Philippe's mama is raising her voice and Philippe is backing up. He sinks so far into his coat he could touch Argentina and he wedges himself between the wall and the couch and then his mama is barreling forward, both arms out, ready to give him the hug of his life. The social worker grabs for Mrs. Brown but she shakes her off. "All you people are ruining my boy!" she screeches.

This is when Mrs. Salvatore steps in and Mrs. Brown slaps her across the cheek. You can hear Mrs. Salvatore breathe in sharply and see her lose her balance.

"Mrs. Brown!" cries the social worker, grabbing

for the woman's hands, then Mrs. Salvatore pushes us under her wings and herds us up the steps and outside. I hear a little sob from Philippe, or maybe he is just clearing grit from his throat, and that is the exact moment I get it.

I understand how if I had Philippe's mama, I might want to hide in my coat, too.

49

This is what it's like to lose your mum.

You have this hollow place inside that never gets filled no matter how hard you try. It's like somebody scraped out your insides and left only bones to hold you together.

You know you have a hole in your life and everyone else does not. If you were only good enough when you were little, maybe she wouldn't have left. Maybe if you didn't cry so much when you were a baby or maybe if you didn't spit out your peas or maybe if you weren't such a grumpy bear, maybe then she would have stayed.

Or maybe if you tried harder in school so you could make something of yourself (like she did), maybe then she would come back.

Maybe, maybe, maybe—always the maybes.

I remember playing hide-and-seek when I was little and hiding in the lilac bushes on one of her visits and she hid behind the maple tree, then she ran and hid in the chokecherries, then she was in the car driving away.

The only thing that really helps is the mad you use to push the sad feelings away. But it's like blocking out the sun. You cover your eyes, but the glare is always there.

As we walk home from the Church of Our Risen Lord and I am thinking about all of this, I almost tell Philippe that this is what it's like to lose your mum.

But I have a feeling he already knows.

50

It turns out that Philippe has had the most interesting life of anyone I have ever known. This is what happens when your mother earns her living playing pool—you tend to travel a lot.

Here's where he's lived:

1. A car
2. A motel room beside the highway
3. The back office of a diner
4. The sleeping cab of an eighteen-wheeler
5. A camper

"You're kidding."

"Am not."

I buy Connecticut and roll again and land on Jail,

but Just Visiting. I have decided to try and be nicer to him after meeting his mama, and also my new plan means I am going to need more help.

Trying harder with Philippe is rough going, though. My skin prickles just watching him in his coat, and I get all riled up when he gives me another Monopoly lesson. I am ready to quit after ten minutes.

"Nobody ever lives in a car, Philippe. Maybe they go on long car rides or take vacations, but they don't *live* in a car."

"Shows what you know, Rosie."

I roll the dice, land on Community Chest, turn over a Get Out of Jail Free card, and take it. "For how long, then?"

"All summer." He shakes his head so his pale curls fall in his eyes. He restacks all the property cards. "And it wasn't a vacation." He buys Marvin Gardens. "We only went to the beach on rainy days, when we could sneak in."

"Well, what did you do the rest of the time?" I roll, landing on New York.

"I'd explore. I met a man who knew how to draw maps and juggle bottles and he showed me how to do both, and a lady who could stand so still you'd think she was made of marble. She taught me how." He puts his arm up like he is the Statue of Liberty. He is very convincing.

164

"Then we lived in the back of Pete's eighteen-wheeler while my mama played pool in Portland. When they broke up, we moved on. He's the one who taught my mama how to pick locks."

Philippe shakes the dice, lands on Pacific, and immediately puts a house on it.

Because I am skinny as I am and always interested in food, I ask, "What do you eat when you live like that?"

He counts his money and restacks it. "You put ice in the sink at the motel. That gives you a refrigerator. You microwave macaroni and cheese—a lot. Sometimes when you're driving you see an orchard and you steal peaches, and then you have your fruit. If you use your imagination, you can pretend it's a piece of pie."

Things have been bad in my life but never so bad I had to pretend a peach was pie. "Well, what about school?"

"I only went sometimes."

It turns out Philippe has dabbled at school the way my papa used to dabble at crossword puzzles—a little bit, once in a while, so he never got very good at it. "Well, don't you get in trouble for not going?"

"Not if they don't catch you. It's pretty hard to keep up with someone who moves so much. It's not much fun going to school anyway, because when you move around, you get really far behind."

I would like to wring his mama's neck. All that

moving, no wonder he doesn't know how to act half the time.

We go around the board once more. Then I casually bring up the subject I want to get to. "I'm riding back to Swanson's."

"Well, don't think that I'm going back there, not ever again." He throws the dice, scowls.

"But I need you, and besides, I need help catching a snake. I have a new plan to distract Swanson."

His eyes widen. "I hate snakes." He lands on Board-walk.

"But it will toughen you up, Philippe. Friends do things for each other. You never had a friend before, so you don't know."

I roll the dice.

"I have so had friends. Stop saying that." He narrows his eyes until they are slivers of steel.

"You are lying. I can tell you never had a friend before me. Now, do you want to help me or not? I have a really good idea. If you ever had a dog, Philippe, you'd do anything to get him back."

"Shut up, Rosie. You're still acting like you're the only one who ever lost a dog. Well, you're not."

"*You* shut up." I close my eyes, try to act bored. Truth is, I don't bother thinking much about other people and their dogs. I only have room in my heart for one.

"I had a dog once," he says, rolling again, this time landing on my property, which unfortunately I haven't put a house on yet.

"I found him in Atlantic City hiding in some newspapers on the side of the road."

I sit up. Grit sifts through the window and I hold my breath until Philippe continues: "I was walking around the boardwalk one night while my mama was playing pool and there he was—little and nearly bald—shivering like he was in snow. But it was summer and very hot. I got a blanket and wrapped him up and carried him back to the camper."

I search for a cool spot in the rug with my toes. "What happened?"

"I fed him milk from the cap of a Coke bottle. I rubbed him down with a blanket every few minutes." He stops. He unbuttons another button. "Did you ever see the movie *One Hundred and One Dalmatians*, where Roger rubs the newborn pup with an old blanket and it brings him back to life? Well, that's what I kept doing. Only it didn't work. He lived for three days. He was sick when I got him and he just got sicker. I named him Jasper. My mama said good thing he went like that because we couldn't keep him anyway."

I notice how small Philippe looks in that wool coat. Suddenly I have the feeling I would like to kiss him.

This is a surprising thought, since I can't remember ever having had it with anybody else. Just a day ago, I could've bitten his mama's head off for saying I was Philippe's girlfriend, and now I am wondering if he has ever had the thought about kissing me. Probably he has, because if I am thinking it, then he must be, too.

I roll the dice, move to Water Works, and buy it. I wait for him to look up. When he does, I lean over with my eyes closed, but I miss and hit his cheek and he jumps up and says, "Aw, Rosie, what'd you do that for?"

I jump back. "Nothing, I wasn't doing anything." My ears burn and I try and think of something to say, but I can't. I roll the dice, land on North Carolina, and buy it, even though I don't like the greens.

I don't tell him that kissing doesn't feel like much anyway.

It's disappointing, like dill pickles that are sweet.

51

"Where's the flashlight?" Philippe asks.

I pull Harry's new one out of my back pocket.

"Hold it up, Rosie," he says before I hardly have a chance to turn it on. "You keep moving it."

"All right," I snap. "Just do it."

We are at the top of the stairs leading down to the dirt-floored cellar under our apartment building. Philippe is sticking a thin file into the padlock on the door. This is a very good lock and he has to jab it for five minutes before we hear the click.

"Well, that took forever," I snort, looking down into the dark hole, kept locked for years because the exterminator can't get rid of the snakes that slither into the crawl space under Eddie's Barbershop every time it rains.

"How about saying *good job* or something like that?" Philippe is very sharp since I tried to give him the kiss.

I make myself stop thinking about that and wave the light, but the beam isn't strong enough to reach the bottom.

"Hold this." I hand Philippe the worn-out little suitcase with metal clasps that Harry keeps under his bed. It is the perfect size.

Philippe steps closer to the edge and looks down. "Isn't there a light?"

"If we turn it on, someone might see." I pick up my snake stick and step down the damp steps. Philippe bumps the suitcase against the wall. The old handle squeaks.

"Shush," I snap, already frustrated that he doesn't know better.

Philippe takes a couple more steps and stops. "Rosie, I—I don't want to do this. I'm going back."

"We're not even at the bottom, and you promised. If you ever had a friend before, you'd help me."

"You keep saying that. I already told you I have so had friends." He sinks further into his coat.

"Well, I don't believe you." The flashlight flickers and I hit it against my thigh until it beams a steady light. "Otherwise, you'd help me." I give him my meanest look, which I'm sure he can see even in the dark, and step down. I have come too far to quit now, with or without Philippe.

The dirt floor is soft under my sneakers, like beach

sand, and the air is cool and wet and hard to breathe. Cobwebs hang like low clouds.

"What's that smell?" Philippe grabs my arm. Already I hear a whine in his voice. I don't know anything about if snakes leave a smell. *The World Book of Unbelievable and Spectacular Things* gives directions for making snake sticks and tells you all about the life cycle of boa constrictors and how to keep them from squeezing the life out of you, but not much else. Snakes probably leave a smell if there are a lot of them, but I keep this thought to myself.

The flashlight quits again—Harry bought the cheapest one at Walmart after yelling at me that I lost his— and I whack it against my leg. There is no other light, except for a sliver of sun that pushes through a hole in the foundation. Something crunches under my feet. Philippe tugs my shirt. I push him away and head for a pile of old wood.

"Harry says snakes hide. If I was a snake, I'd go behind this wood." I pull at one of the boards and accidentally spew a dark wet burst of sawdust into the air.

Philippe covers his nose with the sleeve of his coat. "I really hate snakes. One crawled in the camper once." His breath is hot and ragged against my neck.

I wince. I can't believe I wanted to kiss this boy. "Why are you such a lily-liver, Philippe? When you're afraid of something, *you're supposed to do it anyway.* That's how you get over being afraid."

He turns and starts walking back to the stairs. "No, you're supposed to pay attention if your stomach warns you something is too stupid for words."

I am incensed. "Don't you see? I don't care about anything more than my dog. If you had a true-blue friend like Augustus, you would do anything to bring him home—even this." I pause; my chest heaves. "It's a *really good plan*, Philippe." I don't tell him I'm a little fuzzy about how the whole thing will work.

He stops. Except for the rising and falling of his chest, he is still. "All right," he finally whispers, turning back, "I'll stay, but only because I had a dog once. And I'm not touching a snake, so don't ask me."

I nod and reach for another piece of wood. There's an old door leaning on its side, and under that a pallet, and then a sawhorse, and then a darker, ranker musky smell, which I try and ignore. Another old door leans directly against the stone foundation. "When I pull it away, you shine the light."

"What if there's a snake?" Philippe's whisper has a tremble in it.

"I'll use this," I snap. I hold up the snake stick, try to get my breathing right, and pull.

There's no snake.

God's bones.

52

A few minutes later, when I see the size of the thing wedged between the wall and the oil burner, I think it's a bike tire.

Philippe backs up. I grab his coat and hold him still.

"Rosie, it's a rattler." His voice is a hoarse whisper. "I've read about them."

Chills rise up my neck. I am transfixed by the thick coils, big around as a rolling pin. Harry's suitcase might not be wide enough.

"We don't have rattlers around here," I whisper, my voice thin and far away like it belongs to somebody else. "See those yellow stripes? It's a garter snake."

"You got to be crazy to go for one that big." Philippe turns and heads for the stairs.

"Get back here," I croak. I try to muffle my fury so I don't scare the snake, but this isn't easy to do. "Here, take the flashlight and hold it up."

"But, Rosie, that snake's gigantic."

I could jump down his throat. *I would do anything for my dog, even this.*

Quietly I raise the snake stick, shaped like a perfect Y, over my head. *Don't make a sound, slowly, slowly, slowly,* I tell myself, and I thrust the stick, fast as a bullet, aiming so I can trap the snake just behind the head.

This snake must not have seen anybody in a dozen years—or however long snakes live—because it doesn't startle and it doesn't move until my stick pins it to the floor. Then it whips its thick tail back and forth—*back and forth*—lashing against my shins, thrashing against Philippe's coat.

"Get it, get it, get it!" Philippe screams.

"Quick, the suitcase!" My voice is dry as toast.

Philippe waves the light. "It's over there." The snake twists under the stick, and the whole length of it writhes out from behind the oil burner.

"*Over there?*" I look behind me.

Philippe points to the stairs.

"Well, *go get it.*" I am at the boiling point as Philippe goes back for the suitcase, tripping a little over his coat.

I sink to my knees to try to keep from losing my balance.

"Here," says Philippe after about a million years, and he holds the suitcase out, only of course I can't take it because my hands are tight on the snake stick.

"*Open it, open it, open it.*" I hold tighter as the snake writhes.

I think about this for a long time later—how the sound of the latches snapping open was very loud and why I didn't brace myself just like you do in a horror movie when you know the monster is under the bed. But I don't brace myself, and when Philippe unsnaps the latches, one after the other, I jump and loosen my grip on the stick just the tiniest bit and the snake thrashes away in one powerful thrust and disappears into a space in the stone foundation.

At first all I can do is kneel in the dirt. Then I stand, breathless with fury. Something twists inside me. I whip the flashlight away from Philippe.

"You are the worst friend ever!" I scream, not caring if anyone can hear us all the way down here. "You are no help at all, so you might as well *just go home.*"

Philippe sinks into his coat a little more and watches his black high-tops. His chest rises and falls. Then, without looking at me, he turns and plods along the dirt floor until he reaches the steps.

"And, Rosie?" he calls, looking back at me. "I've heard of dumb ideas before, but this is the dumbest plan *ever in the history of the universe.*"

Then he feels his way up to the top, opens the door, and slams it behind him. The padlock thumps, and I am left in the darkness alone.

53

Fine.

I will catch a snake *myself*, I will take it out to Swanson's *by myself*, then I will get my dog, *all by myself*.

I pull my shirt over my nose and remind myself that plans that are a little fuzzy around the edges work best when you do them *all by yourself* so you can improvise.

My breath is slow, steady, hot. I pick up the suitcase with one hand and the snake stick and flashlight with the other and begin feeling my way around the cellar walls.

Harry told me about the crawl space that runs under the barbershop, and also about how snakes like it there because it is cramped and cool and damp. Folks kept baskets of apples and squash and potatoes in there before anybody had refrigerators—that's how old this building is.

My flashlight blinks off and I whack it back on. The ceiling in the crawl space is waist-high and cobwebs make long sweeping curtains. I am not this brave.

I hear my mum say I will never amount to anything. Grizzlies roar behind my ears. My head throbs.

I push the cobwebs aside and pull myself through the narrow space, navigating with my hands, pressing forward, feeling something lumpy poke at my hip.

The musky smell is strong. Harry says there are snakes in here, but where? I shine my flashlight into the dark space. There is a pile of stones on the far side and, thanks to a chink in the foundation, a little light. My shoulders ache from crouching.

I begin pulling away the stones, shining my light into the crevices. After a few minutes I give up. There is no snake.

Slowly, inch by inch, I crawl around the floor, feeling into every corner, touching cobwebs, running my fingers along damp foundation stone. The scabs on my knee open and I should probably stop and clean the dirt out, but I don't. The damp air fills my chest like cotton. Cobwebs cling to my cheek.

Finally, behind an old oilcan on a little ledge I see a snake no bigger than a ruler. I'm not sure if it is big enough to scare anyone, but at least it will fit in the suitcase.

I'm in one of those slow-motion movies, reaching behind me, picking up the snake stick, but there's not enough room over my head to get it to swing right.

My fingers yell at me not to even think about trying this without the snake stick—these snakes may not be poisonous, but maybe they bite.

And my toes snap: *How will you explain a snakebite to Harry?*

I tell all the parts of me to shut up, and I raise my arms and silently take three tiny steps forward.

When I pounce, I am catlike, and I land in the tight space with my fingers outstretched, my nails out, and wrap my fingers around the slender body just behind the head and clamp hard, pinning the snake to the ledge. It thrashes and whips its thin tail around, exposing its cream-colored belly, which oddly reminds me of Philippe's hair. I reach down and grab it behind the neck. It opens its mouth. Its eyes glint.

My shoulders shudder. My breath is lost somewhere in my belly. I concentrate on holding the snake behind the head as tightly as I can. I remind myself that I have a very good plan, that distraction is the thing, and that if I can scare Swanson enough, she might not notice if I run off with my dog.

Forcing myself not to scream, I lift the snake and drop it into the suitcase, snap the lid shut, and sit back on my heels, panting.

I did it.

Slowly the roaring in my ears stills, the grizzlies drift off, and when I find my breath again, I begin the long crawl out of the cramped dark space, dragging the suitcase behind me, feeling the lumpiness sliding back and forth inside.

I beam.

I am magnificent.

54

I tell Harry he is dumber than a bag of hammers. This doesn't go over well.

"Now!" he bellows.

I wrap myself deep in my army blanket, tighter this time so there's no way he can unroll me.

"I am not going to the doctor. You can't make me."

He stomps over, grabs the blanket. I roll tighter, pressing the edges together like pie dough. My bed braces itself. My toes wince.

"I can't keep enough ice in the house for all those headaches. Now get up."

Harry pulls. I grab the bedpost. He yanks so hard the room spins and I flip, but this time he catches me before I hit the floor.

"Now!" he growls into my ear.

*　*　*

The doctor's office is on the first floor of one of the old houses on Main Street. It has a little sign on a post that says DR. MONROE WALTERS. It swings when you open the gate. Inside, everything smells like Pine-Sol. Aluminum blinds clack when the breeze picks up.

I yank my sleeve from Harry's grasp. "You don't have to pull me." When my papa brought me here, we'd do the *Highlights* puzzles together so I wouldn't worry about the shots. Now I push those memories away and consider how long a snake can survive in a suitcase.

When the nurse calls me in, Harry stands up. "I don't need you to come," I snap.

"Right," he mutters, his ears turning red.

The nurse hands me a paper johnny—"open in the back"—and she makes me sit on the chair and wait. The clock ticks, my johnny rustles, my head throbs. The sun is out—it would be a perfect day to get my Gloaty Gus.

Hornets whirl.

The nurse comes back and makes me stand on the scale. I hold the back of my johnny tight while she pushes the weight bar further to the left. "Can that really be all you weigh?"

I snap, "You would, too, if you had to eat sardine sandwiches all the time." The nurse giggles nervously, unsure if I am telling the truth. She checks my eyes to see if I am lying, then she gathers up her thermometer and blood pressure cuff and leaves. I snort, pleased that I have put Harry in the worst light possible.

When the doctor comes in, his hands are very cold and smell of antiseptic. He checks my throat, feels both sides of my neck, and looks in my ears long enough to see Tibet. "Tell me about the headaches," he says, shining his flashlight in my eyes.

I shrug.

"Show me where it hurts."

I point to my head.

"Yes, I understand that. In one spot or all over?"

I make my hand sweep across my entire head, back and forth, up and down.

"I see—that bad, huh? When do you get them? In school?"

I nod—especially in school, but now all the time.

The doctor sits on his little rolling stool and points to the eye chart on the wall. "Read the third row."

I read it perfectly. He presses his thumbs into the skin on both sides of my nose, deep against my sinuses. "Does that hurt?"

I shake my head. He types something in his computer. "We'll get you a blood test, and some more tests after that if we need to. But I have a question I want to ask you."

I hold my breath. The clock ticks.

"Headaches can originate for all sorts of reasons, and stress can be a factor. Your father's stroke and your feelings about that could certainly contribute."

I glare at him while tigers shred my heart.

"I don't need a blood test." I pull the johnny so hard it rips and I have to hold it together until he finally leaves.

I just need my dog. Why doesn't anyone understand that?

The doctor is talking to Harry when I walk past his office, and Harry answers, "Well, I had planned on being retired"—*mumble*—"and playing poker"—*mumble mumble*—"if you want to know the truth."

I creep back. The doctor's voice is thinner than Harry's gruff Marines growl. "Sometimes life doesn't work out the way you want, you know that as well as I do, Harry." *Mumble mumble.* "It may be too much for you."

My grandpa clears his throat. *Mumble mumble mumble.* "The ice cubes?"

"They do absolutely nothing."

"That's what I told her," Harry says.

I scoff.

"Now, visiting her father, that might help." *Mumble.* "She's stuffing all those emotions inside. But I will order the other tests, just to be sure."

Harry snorts. *Mumble mumble.* "We don't need more

tests. In my day we filled a hot water bottle and went to bed."

Mumble mumble mumble. Then: "You need to get her mother back in the picture, anyway. You're not a young man—too old to be raising a young girl like that."

My breath bursts inside me and I let the door slam behind me. I live inside one of those snow globe things and everybody is always shaking it up.

55

It rains. For three days it rains so hard that water pours over our streets, pushing leaves and branches and grit along the roads, clogging culverts and turning Main Street into a choppy ocean.

Water rises to the top step at the barbershop and Eddie piles sandbags out front. Trash cans float and empty soda cans bounce along new rivers that rush down our sidewalks. Potholes split the cement outside the donut shop, and the noon train makes a wet slapping sound as it sloshes into town.

You can't ride the Blackbird through raging rivers, so I have to wait days to get my Gloaty Gus. This makes my head throb even more and I jump down Harry's throat when he comes home with half a dozen new tins of sardines and a box of saltines.

I punch airholes in the little suitcase so the snake can breathe and hide it in the back of my closet, where Harry never goes. My *World Book* is no help on snake care, so I sprinkle drops of water and catch a spider and a couple of ants in the pantry and slide them inside.

I hear my dog whining in the middle of the night—a whisper on the wind—and my heart cramps from all the wanting. In the morning my chest muscles ache. I twirl my spoon through my cornflakes, not liking them one bit more than I did when I moved in with Harry. I let them float until they are too soggy to eat and throw them in the trash.

I go back to bed and pull the army blanket to my nose. Elephants stomp behind my eyes. The rain thrums against my window and looking out is like opening your eyes at the bottom of a swimming pool.

Harry walks through the soaking rain to check on me. He doesn't bring up Mr. Peterson or the work I'm supposed to do in the notebook. Instead, he carries our little television into my room, and while he is plugging it in, he says, "You should come with me to visit your father. The doctor says it might help."

I dive deeper under my army blanket. The hornets whir.

"Acting like it never happened is making it worse, Rosie."

"Go away." When my grandpa leaves for the donut shop, I wet one of our thin towels with ice water and cover my eyes.

Immediately the hornets hum themselves to sleep, which shows how little Harry really knows about anything.

56

"I love fishing. I never went before, but I know I just love it."

Cynthia hops a little when she bounces down the steps and her voice rises at the end of her sentences: "I'm as happy as a flower bursting in the sun about going fishing. How about you, Rosie? Do you like fishing as much as me?"

I snort—no, I do not. Now that the rain has slowed to a drizzle, I am in an awful rush to get my dog, but Harry is making me carry the tackle box and the rod he keeps in his closet. "That boy needs to fish."

I can't help the screech that flies from my mouth. I don't care if he needs to learn to fish or not. I am not even talking to Philippe, who right now is huddled in his coat and won't look at me as we march outside. He is still mad about the cellar. My toes sizzle every time I even *think* about him saying the snake plan is the dumbest idea in the history of the world.

Plus, Philippe has been playing Monopoly with Cynthia—I know, because Mrs. Salvatore called me a lazybones and asked why I wasn't playing with them. Fine, let him be friends with Cynthia—who cares?— but doesn't he notice the nest in her hair and all the scratching?

Harry hands Philippe a pair of binoculars and Cynthia an umbrella that used to be my papa's. She opens it and Philippe walks under.

"Don't you know she cheats at everything?" I hiss, making my voice snap like a rubber band.

"Not as much as you do, Rosie."

I kick at Philippe, but he moves closer to Cynthia. I snort and Harry snarls what am I being so snarky about?

Our first stop is the toolshed so Harry can get the shovel and we can dig worms. With all the rain, I haven't had a chance to hide my bike after I got it out of the dumpster.

As soon as Harry gets the door open, Cynthia bursts: "Wow, it's your bike! Did they catch you, Rosie? My mama's old boyfriend got caught stealing from a dumpster and he had to go to pay a ticket and maybe even go to jail for a while."

Harry glances quickly over to me, then steps closer to the Blackbird, which I left leaning against his old ladder. He coughs a few times to get the frog out of his throat, then runs his hands over the crunched metal basket and squeezes until his knuckles go white. I hold my breath. Cynthia tries to climb on. Tarantulas march behind my ears.

"Get off," Harry barks at her, and he throws me the shovel. When I just stand there waiting for him to say something about how my bike is back home, abracadabra (but crunched to smithereens from getting thrown in the dumpster), he changes the subject and growls, "Hurry up, we need two dozen worms and I don't have all day."

He pokes the kickstand with the toe of his boot. When it slips down, he wheels the Blackbird outside while I try not to explode. He grunts as he straightens the seat. "Come hold the handlebars," he tells Philippe.

I push hard on the shovel, and the ground is so soft from the rain my foot sinks to Australia. The dirt is rich and brown out by the toolshed and a half-dozen worms come up wriggling in the first load.

"I can put the worms on," says Cynthia, leaving the umbrella and skipping over to me. "I've never done it before but I watched my mama's old boyfriend do it once and he did it really slow so I could see how he stuck the hook in so I know I can do it and I don't get sad about things like that, I just close my eyes, so can I do it?" she says, turning back to Harry. "I always wanted to catch a fish my whole life."

My grandpa bends the seat straight. "You can if you shut your trap. You talk too much."

Cynthia is quiet for a minute—and it is a peaceful relief, I can tell you that, but you can see her eyes popping from the strain and you get the feeling you know what Noah felt when he wanted to hold back the flood.

"Hold it straight," Harry tells Philippe, and then he goes inside the shed and comes out with his old toolbox, gets down on his knees—you can hear his bones groan—and tightens the wheel.

He must have practiced when this was my papa's bike because Harry doesn't strip threads the way I do. He tightens the kickstand and then the seat.

He tries to straighten the crunched fender, but Philippe isn't holding tight enough and the bike slips and Harry jabs his knee. "How many times do I need to tell you to take that coat off," he growls. "It's ridiculous."

Way deep inside me my heart pays no attention at all to how mad I am at Philippe, and it swells with a thousand *oh no*s. I hold my breath as Philippe locks down: he stiffens, his face goes pale as a bedsheet, and his jaws clamp shut.

"But he hardly ever takes it off," Cynthia says, whining a little.

"Now!" Harry roars. "You can't fish with it on, either."

Philippe does nothing for at least a minute and I am just starting to think we have a showdown on our hands when he reaches up and slowly loosens the big black buttons. The coat slips to the ground.

I stop digging. Harry clears his throat a few times. "In my day when you were afraid of the dark, you went out at midnight and dug potatoes. You didn't hide in your coat all the time."

Philippe shivers. He is thin as a baby bird. He tries to hold the bike straight, but without his coat he loses his power. Harry looks at me and then over to Cynthia. Finally, after about a thousand years, he says, "Oh, for Pete's sake, it's probably going to rain again anyway—put it back on."

My heart takes a deep breath. My toes relax.

"I won't have to go swimming, will I?" says Cynthia, bouncing over to help hold my bike. "I don't like to swim. My mama's boyfriend—the same one who taught me about worms—he made me go swimming one day even when I told him I didn't know how and he told me do the dog paddle out to the middle and then he pushed me under so I would learn real fast to hold my breath, but I almost drowned. You won't make me swim, will you?"

Harry's ears twitch. He stands up and looks at her a long while. Then he grumbles, "When you fish, you don't swim. It scares the fish."

My grandpa is still shaking his head when we set off for the pond.

Fishing is a disaster, as you can imagine. On the way home, Philippe and Cynthia walk together under the umbrella. I plod through the drizzle with my head down.

Harry makes me carry the fish—a scrawny perch that Cynthia caught and now we're going to have to eat, *God's bones*. I rub my throbbing temples.

My grandpa doesn't mention throwing my bike into the dumpster ever again, but halfway home, when the sky opens up and it begins to pour, he takes off his old fishing hat and puts it on my head.

57

A yellow envelope, a little greasy and stuffed full, sits between us in Harry's truck. It's filled with cash, mostly ones and fives—donut money.

"It's not like he's done anything to earn it." I say it with my snarkiest voice. You could slice meat with the sharpness of it.

"Stop talking." Harry drums his thumb on the steering wheel as we head out to Mr. Peterson's house.

Mrs. Salvatore is boxing donuts behind the counter when we bump through a new pothole in front of the JACK'S DONUTS sign.

After the doctor had that talk about Harry being too old to raise me, Mrs. Salvatore agreed to work a couple of hours when Harry needs time off to do the things you do when you have a grandchild—buy real toothpaste and get rid of the baking-soda-and-salt mix you keep on the sink, replace the cornflakes with brown sugar oatmeal and your worn-out towels with a few new ones from Walmart, hang curtain rods, fix the clanking pipes in the tub, buy window fans and bubble bath, make sure your life insurance is up to date, get a will done.

In return for this help at the donut shop, Harry does some dad things for the boy who never had a father. This explains the fishing trip. I roll my eyes.

Harry flips the radio to the sports talk station as we drive to where the roads narrow and the houses get smaller, then onto another road and up a pencil-thin driveway where the grass hasn't been mowed and a late crop of dandelions bursts like a million tiny suns. Mr. Peterson stands high on a ladder, pulling soggy leaves out of his gutters.

Harry turns the engine off. He thumps his thumb on the steering wheel—one, two, three . . . eight, nine, ten. "Get moving."

"I already told you there's nothing in the notebook. So why are we even doing this?"

"I said we were coming today. If you chose not to do the work, that's your problem. Now go." He pours more coffee into his GONE FISHING mug and leans back, pulling his hat low to block the sun. It has been many days since we've had to blink brightness out of our eyes.

58

It is not every day you go to a teacher's house.

This one has the same stained-glass jeweled windows up and down the sides of the front door that we had on Maple Street, and it is trimmed by juniper bushes, the kind that trap fat snowflakes in winter.

There's a barn, a tree house high in a pine off to the side, and a big yellow Labrador on the porch, its tail already wagging. Laughter rolls out of the tree house and everybody-do-the-twist music bebops out the window.

The scene makes a happy picture and for just a moment I breathe in the joyfulness of it all. I see where Mr. Peterson gets his tra-la-las.

* * *

When he notices me, he gives me a little salute and climbs down. "I am very interested to see what you have written, Rosie."

The trees all around his yard are so big their branches touch. I kick a clump of dandelions. I let my silence speak for itself.

"I see," he says, reaching for the notebook, glancing over at Harry's truck. He wipes his fingers on his overalls, opens the cover, and hands it right back. "You know, Rosie, writing can light a fire. Writing like this can light *your life* on fire."

I kick another clump of yellow. *God's bones*, he sounds like a teacher.

He prods the dandelions back up with his foot.

I snort and give him the envelope, which he leafs through and hands back without taking the money.

"I don't have time for this, Rosie. I would only take an extra student in my class who wanted to make something of herself, who was willing to put in the effort. I am very demanding, and since you're not willing to do the work, good luck in Mrs. Barrett's class."

I wince.

"Yes?" he asks gently.

I scrunch my face, trying to come up with something. Finally, I shove the envelope back to him. "Harry wants you to take the money. He says he hired you to tutor me and you've done your part."

"I haven't done anything, not yet." He waits for some kind of answer but I don't have one to give and I concentrate on my sneakers, listening for the far-off rumbling of the train heading into town.

Mr. Peterson reaches for the ladder. "You won't know the potential in yourself, Rosie, until you learn how to look inside to find it. Writing can help you do that."

Hornets whirl themselves into a frenzy.

As he climbs, I'm left holding the notebook and the envelope stuffed with cash. His sneakers squeak against the rails, probably from all the holes in the soles. Across the lawn, his twins have poked their heads out of the tree house to watch.

I have that funny feeling you get when you wake up after you weren't expecting to fall asleep on the bus, a little dizzy and embarrassed and everyone is watching.

"That's it?" Harry jumps a little when I stomp back to the truck, kicking all the dandelions in my path. He has nodded off. There must be a blue moon tonight because Harry never naps.

I sizzle as I toss the envelope at him.

"He won't let me in his class."

Harry shoves the envelope into his shirt pocket and backs down the driveway. "Finally, a teacher with sense."

My head pounds; a thousand barracudas swarm behind my eyes.

When we reach our apartment, I head straight for the ice cubes.

59

At six o'clock the phone rings.

I let it go until it stops.

I pull the army blanket over my head. The wool smells musty from all the rain and I doze off, feeling my papa near me telling me something about Augustus, over and over like a jackhammer.

I jolt awake. The phone is ringing again. Harry yells, "Aren't you going to answer that thing?"

I bury my head under my pillow. When the telephone rings a third time, Harry picks it up and mumbles something. I roll myself tighter in the army blanket and close my eyes.

I want to talk to my papa about a lot of things, like how to get the light on my bike to stay on and how I am going to wait *another day* for Harry to stop keeping such a close watch on me so I can go rescue the true-blue friend of my soul.

I might mention Philippe and how we are not really friends anymore. My papa would understand how annoying he is, and also how maybe you don't always want to be friends with the girl who doesn't brush her hair, and why do you have to?

Harry stomps in with his frown the size of Saturn. He's got the ledger he uses to make sense of the donut shop profits, which lately haven't been adding up. My grandpa doesn't believe in computers.

"She wants to visit."

I sit up. "*You invited her?* I can't believe you'd do that."

"She's your mother. You talk, even if it's hard, even if you don't want to."

"You're going to let her take me away? I thought you wanted me. . . ." My voice trails off, footprints in the snow.

Harry stares at me like I have two heads. "You haven't seen her in a year. She wants to visit. That's all."

I have so many things to say to my mum I don't know where to start, but believe me, I will give her bucketloads.

It turns out when the phone rings half an hour later, she is the one who talks first: "Rosalita?"

"It's Rosie."

She pauses. "Yes." She stops, takes a breath. "I called to say I'm coming for a visit at the end of the month."

The knot in my belly tightens.

She takes another breath.

"I would like to plant the idea of moving you out here with me."

"But my dog!" I can't help the screech that flies out of my mouth.

My mum groans. "Rosalita, I am sick of you asking about that dog. It would never remember you at this point anyway. I'm sure it's settled in with a new family and it would be very cruel to take it away."

I double over from the sword in my belly and wrap myself tighter in my army blanket. I don't want to consider this.

Except for her breathing, my mum is quiet. Then she says, "I would just like you to make something of your life, and I don't see that happening in that town. Your father never wanted to leave, but I did. You can, too, Rosalita."

"It's Rosie."

"Yes."

"I'm fine here," I tell her.

"Yes, I understand that, Rosalita. But I'm offering you a golden ticket—one your grandfather could never give you. You do want to amount to something, don't you?"

But I'd never find my dog.

"Did you hear me, Rosalita?"

The early-evening train rumbles through town. The floor shakes. My toes brace themselves.

"This is so frustrating, Rosalita." My mum breathes sharply. "I just don't understand you. That dog smelled and it drooled and it jumped out the windows, for God's sake."

And he was the best friend of my soul.

"Rosalita, can you hear me? You could amount to something if only—"

"My name is *Rosie!*" I scream, interrupting her tight hard voice, finding my own.

60

When the line goes dead, I pull my knees to my face and hug them.

After a while, I dump two trays of ice cubes into an empty bread bag (which Harry makes me recycle) and climb onto the fire escape, but Philippe and Cynthia are already out there playing Monopoly, so I crawl back into my room and slam the window shut.

That night I dream about my Augustus getting tangled in my wheel as I fly the Blackbird home. Puddles everywhere, an ocean racing through the streets, I can't get us through the roaring flood in front of me, I can't get us home.

My heart skids out of my chest—*thump thump thump*. I try to breathe, but my lungs take in only water.

I wake. The night outside my window is licorice black.

It has begun to pour once more.

PART III

61

I make myself tough as boiled bear and march the Blackbird past Cynthia and Philippe.

The snake thuds softly in the suitcase. The handle squeaks.

Cynthia rushes after me. "My mama says it's going to pour really hard again today, do you know that, Rosie? There's going to be so much rain you could drown, maybe even it's going to hail. Did you know you could die from getting hit on the head by hail? My mama told me that happened to a man she read about. It was in a book about crazy things that can happen to you." She points at my helmet. "Is that why you're wearing that ski hat under there, because it's going to hail?"

My ears twist with fury. "Get your nose out of my business, Cynthia."

Harry believes in sharing my papa's umbrella and now I have to watch the two of them dragging it through the mud while the volcano roars inside me.

"Where are you going with that?" Cynthia reaches for the suitcase.

I yank it away. "Leave me alone, Cynthia."

"Yes, what *are* you doing with that suitcase?" Philippe snorts in a way that lets me know exactly how furious he still is about me calling him a baby and everything else that happened in the basement. His coat is unbuttoned and nearly hanging off him.

Seething, I crush his bones with my eyes. *Don't you dare tell her.*

He hardly blinks. "Yeah, well, it's the dumbest idea ever. I already told you that."

The hornets can hardly believe he is saying this. They swarm.

You can see the question in Cynthia's eyes. She takes a step closer to the suitcase. "My mama says I can be with you."

"Well, you can't. Now go away. And I can't believe you want to be friends with someone so stupid he hides in that huge coat all the time." My oatmeal churns in my belly, and my papa says in my head how maybe I am going too far to take it back.

Cynthia crosses her arms over her chest. She is wearing her tie-dyed shirt. "You're a terrible friend, Rosie."

"I am not," I snap, pushing the Blackbird around her.

"Are too," Philippe says, picking up a trash bag filled with old cans and pulling it toward the road. "Worst ever."

Something inside me erupts as I watch them being together. "You are wrong. No one ever called me a terrible friend before, so I don't believe you."

Cynthia turns around. "Oh no? Then how come you don't have any, Rosie. How come?"

62

The snake thuds inside the little suitcase as I pedal furiously past the donut shop. The downpour over the past week washed most of the grit away, but what is left on the road is thick as flour paste.

Harry's wrench bounces in my basket in case the wheel wobbles, and a thin file and screwdriver jab through my back pocket. I have also tied a rope around and around my waist in case Augustus forgets how to follow me home.

I drag my feet to slow down and steer around mounds of wet sand, turning onto a side road and heading up the next. The suitcase bangs against the crunched fender. The rope around my waist tightens when I lean forward to pedal. A garbage truck plows by, spewing greasy puddle water in my face, and I have to pull over and wipe under my goggles.

When I test my brakes, they freeze and won't clamp the tires. My head wants to think about holding Augustus in my arms, but when you have lousy brakes you have to concentrate on the road.

Halfway up the first hill it begins to pour. It is almost impossible to stand up and pedal through the rain when you have a suitcase in your hand, and I wonder about the airholes: *Can snakes drown?* I hear my papa in my head: *You need grit in this life, Rosie*—which is the biggest joke of all in our town because we all have enough grit to taste it in our sleep.

As I start up Swanson's hill, bits of hail form a thin coat of ice on the road and my tires can't grip the pavement. Sharp frozen nails pierce my face. I have to keep taking my hand off the handlebar to wipe my goggles, and this isn't a very good thing to do, because if you've ever ridden your bike through icy grit, you know how slippery it is.

I hold the suitcase tighter. At the top of the last hill my toes sing a few hosannas because Swanson's farm spreads out in front of me and—good news—her jeep isn't in the driveway. I tighten my grip and start downhill. The milk truck flies up behind me, swerving at the last minute, spraying slush, and I cut my wheel hard to the right, flying along the side of the road, dragging my feet to keep from crashing.

A runoff gully cuts into the side of the road and my toes scream, *Hold on!* as we soar across, then tumble and flip over and over until I am splayed on the road and icy gravel slashes my face and sand rips the skin off my elbow.

I see stars. My head throbs. Icy rain pelts my skin. I lie like this for a very long time.

Dizzy and winded—sprawled several feet away from my twisted Blackbird—I wonder if this is how it feels at the end of everything. I open my mouth because my tongue would like a little rain. My toes give up.

The thing about being smashed on the ground like this with your cheek pressed into the wet dirt is you can hear the grinding motor of a big sand truck from far off. It's a deep growling, a snarling rumbling engine sound— and the earth vibrates under you.

I sit up, groaning with dizziness, and flop back down. How long does it take everything to stop whirling?

I lie on the edge of the road, the ground spinning, light-headed as an ant on a merry-go-round. The truck downshifts as it slowly grinds up the steep grade.

Frantically I roll into a clump of prickers, cover my head with my good arm, and wait for the end to come.

When the sand truck finally roars over the hill, it

swerves to dodge my bike and comes so close I feel the heat of the engine in my eyes. I press myself deeper into the wet gravel as it thunders by.

I hear my papa in my head: *You'll never even live if you keep this up.*

63

After a while, I remember the snake.

Harry's suitcase lies open on the far side of the road. I watch bleary-eyed as the rain bounces off the blue satin lining and spatters the ground.

The strap of my helmet cuts into my nose and a knife twists where my elbow used to be. I try to stand, unsteady and swaying. My head roars as gorillas stomp behind my eyes, and when the dizziness is too much, I sink back on the road and watch helplessly as the little snake pokes its head out of the suitcase.

No, no, no.

My legs tremble as I rise to my knees and watch the snake slither toward a clump of pine trees and disappear.

Hornets whirl.

I scream until no sound comes and then all is silent the way things are silent in those old movies Harry watches, silence before the storm.

Get a grip, I breathe in. *Get a grip*, I breathe out.

When I can finally stand long enough to count to fifty, I cradle my arm and pull my dented bike into the bushes.

And then—without a snake, without a plan, and slow as an old retriever who won't run anymore—I begin the long walk to get my dog.

64

I've never broken into someone's house before, but it can't be that different from breaking into a barn.

I hear my papa in my head saying it's a really bad idea.

I hesitate halfway up the driveway and this gives my toes time to gang up on me and refuse to go forward (they will dillydally until the cows come home, they tell me).

I snap at them: *We have no choice.* Swanson isn't home and my dog is in the house, not the barn. *Can't you hear the barking?*

Crows caw and soar into the sopping sky and I use Harry's gruff Marines voice to force all the parts of me to march across the soaked lawn and up the porch steps. My sneakers squeak. My elbow throbs.

Swanson's windows are closed and covered with thick curtains. Two are broken and patched with duct tape.

Inside, I hear my dog jumping and barking, and my heart swells and soars as again and again he howls, and the sweet sound of it is a warm blanket covering all the aching places inside me. I notice that my Gloaty Gus's deep booming tone is missing and a high yelping has taken its place, but no matter, we can get things back to normal as soon as I wrap my arms around the true-blue friend of my soul.

The yelping continues, louder and louder, until it becomes that baying moan that wolves make at the moon.

"Stop barking!" I try to hide the tiniest trace of irritation creeping into my voice because my dog doesn't have the sense to know it's me, but the howling goes on and on and I realize we are going to have to learn to be with each other all over again. My papa told me that newly sheared sheep butt heads because they don't recognize each other, sometimes for the rest of the day. This is a little reassuring, but not much.

The front door is bolted shut. I try all the windows on the porch, but each is locked. Every time I reach up to try and raise a sash, my elbow throbs and I stagger from the dizziness. My dog yelps so much I can't hear myself think. I don't even hear the oil truck rumbling up the driveway until it is almost too late, and I dive into the boxwood bushes on the far side of the porch, groaning from the pain.

From my hiding spot I notice another window on the far side of the house—more narrow, but slightly open—and I will need something to stand on to get up there, so when the oil truck finishes filling the tank, I waste another fifteen minutes finding a rusted folding chair pushed under the porch.

As I wedge the window up with my good arm, my dog breaks up his howling with that high yapping yelp, which hardly sounds like Augustus at all. Then he wails and this makes me wonder what Swanson has done to him. Cradling my arm, I crawl through the window and jump. This is no easy feat with my heart thundering, and I land in a bathroom, banging my elbow on the floor tiles. I moan louder than my dog, I can tell you that.

When I finally stop rolling and gasping, I notice a lacy shower curtain hanging not far from my nose and soft pink wallpaper with little roses. It is not the sort of bathroom I would pick for someone like Swanson, but my papa told me folks are complicated and have many sides to them, so don't think you are so smart until you walk in their shoes for a while.

My dog barks as I stand dizzily and open the bathroom door. It leads into a kitchen with a stuffed sofa, an old black stove, and a metal pail catching water dripping from the ceiling.

Philippe and Cynthia whisper in my head, *Don't you remember she shoots squirrels?* I push them and everything else away—including my mum, who is yelling, *Good God, Rosalita, you'll never amount to anything if you keep this up*—because I'm in a movie now, hurrying toward the one I love.

The yapping is coming from a room at the front of the house and with each step my toes warn me that the barking doesn't sound quite right.

Stop being such a worrywart, I snap, rushing breathlessly toward the door and flinging it open, just like they do in the movies.

65

The ears don't perk up right.

That's the first thing.

He doesn't have that grin that only I can see.

That's the second thing.

He has a white mask painted across his face from a long life, and his eyes don't open.

Those are the third and fourth things.

No one could ever mistake this honey-colored dog for my scruffy Gloaty Gus.

The dog jumps and wails at the ceiling. My heart pounds frantically. Already my toes are screaming, *We warned you*, and my heart is whispering that if the true-blue friend of my soul was here, he would already be in my arms.

The blood roars in my ears. I have been wrong about everything.

* * *

The dog (that is not my dog) backs into the corner and raises the fur along his spine and howls. Blind, he sniffs at me, rushes forward and then backs up, over and over, like a bad movie that doesn't end.

My legs get that shaky feeling you get when you swim too long at the beach. I take a few steps back, my heart hammering. The dog yaps and then edges closer, one paw at a time, sniffing at my shins, trying to figure out who I am, growling more fiercely the closer he gets, and finally lunging at me.

I sprint for the front door.

I've never broken into a house before and I've done it for a dog that isn't mine.

Worse things have happened to me, but right now I can't think what.

66

I freeze.

Swanson stops short. She is already halfway up the porch steps when I fly out the front door and I never even heard her jeep over all the howling.

Wet and trembling, frail, her hunting hat pulled low, her gray eyes large and stunned, she looks like a rabbit about to spring.

The dog (that is not my dog) yelps. The crows in the sopping pine shriek and shoot for the sky. I shiver under my wet clothes, my elbow burns, my heart races, my mouth is very dry. I back into the door. I take many deep breaths to get myself in line. It is the longest few minutes of my life.

The dog (that is not my dog) dashes around me to lean against Swanson and howls. Swanson makes that odd chicken-clucking noise and snaps her fingers and the dog sits and buries his muzzle in her knee. Her thin wrist trembles as she scratches the dog's ears and I realize I've frightened her terribly, which makes me feel even worse about everything.

I hear my papa in my head: *She doesn't have anything and never did.*

My chest tightens from the panic climbing inside me, and my voice is thin when I finally find it. "I came for my dog," I whisper, cradling my elbow, trying to edge around her. "My mum gave him away when my papa went into the hospital and I thought you had him. I saw him here, or at least I thought I heard him. I've been looking for him for a very long time." My voice catches.

Swanson darts around me and steps into the house. Her dog scurries behind her. She slams the door.

A wave of grief rises inside me. My toes clench and I grab the porch column because the earth tilts and I am unsteady on my feet. All this way, and it's not even my Gloaty Gus. Harry is going to wring my neck.

I have just stepped into the rain when Swanson opens the door again. She has taken off her hat and her wet coat and put on a big bulky red sweater (way too hot for summer, but grown-ups are funny in some ways). The honey-colored dog is wedged close to her, panting.

"I didn't mean to scare you," I whisper. "I just miss my dog so much." My voice knots and I brace myself for her to tell me she's already called the police. With my bike crumpled in the bushes and my twisted throbbing elbow, I will have a hard time making it home without help.

Instead, she stares at me so long I feel her searching the very bottom of my heart.

Then she makes that odd chicken-clucking noise and motions me inside.

67

The rain beats a steady thrum while we watch each other. The dog presses his muzzle deeper into Swanson's leg. The house holds its breath.

No one knows where I am.

My papa loved reading *Little Red Riding Hood* ("How could anyone be so stupid to go in that cottage?") and *Hansel and Gretel* ("Those idiotic children!"), and from the time I could toddle along behind him, he warned me not to talk to strangers. Yet here I am, considering following Swanson into her house because it is pouring outside, my bike is crumpled on the side of the road, the skin is hanging off my elbow, my dog isn't here, and I need to call Harry.

Coyotes snarl in my head. Truly I am the biggest idiot in the universe.

Think, think, think, use your head, maybe you'll amount to something.

God's bones. I sound like my mum.

Finally, when each option looks bleaker than the last, I make a decision. I ask if I can use the phone.

Swanson stomps her rain boots a few times on the braided rug by the door and heads inside. Soaked and shivering, I tell myself that things can hardly get worse than they already are.

The holes in my sneakers sift thin trails of sand onto the rough floors as I follow Swanson and her dog into the kitchen, where everything smells like cinnamon.

The honey-colored dog pads past the table slowly, carefully, brushing against a chair, navigating with eyes closed until he finds a rug near the back door, sits, sniffs at me, and whines softly.

Swanson scratches her dog between the ears, fussing with that clucking noise. I figure out her dog is a she. I was wrong about even that.

"I just thought my dog was here," I whisper, feeling any hope I ever had of finding my Gloaty Gus slide to the floor.

68

Swanson is so much smaller when you are up close, not much taller than me.

Her bone face is thin and creased, and when she pulls off her hunting hat, you see her hair is chopped in a floppy boy's cut, like Philippe's.

The dog (that is not my dog) pads over to her and whines and Swanson makes that clucking noise and softly strokes the dog's face, then the dog circles and slowly lies down, dropping her muzzle to the floor. When Swanson pulls a can of cocoa from the cupboard and holds it up, I consider only for a second, then nod. Harry doesn't believe in cocoa.

There's a sign hanging above her stove—yellowed and crimped from heat—that reads COUNT YOUR BLESSINGS.

This seems an odd bit of wisdom for someone like

Swanson, who lives all alone without any friends (that I know of) or family (that I know of) and doesn't talk. How many blessings can she have?

My papa told me one day at the donut shop, "Just because she doesn't talk doesn't mean she's stupid, so don't harden your heart like some people in this town."

I think about this as she hands me a quilt to wrap myself in and sets a steaming mug on the table beside me. She reaches for my elbow, but I pull it away and hold it under the quilt, close to my chest. The dog whines.

No one knows where I am.

The cocoa is very thick with chocolate. I begin planning how I'm going to gloss over what I've done when I talk to Harry.

Next Swanson puts on a pair of thick reading glasses, pulls an onion from her pantry, chops it, and fries it in butter. Surely she will tell Harry everything. I wince as much from the pain in my elbow as from what Harry is going to do to me.

She pulls a frayed tea towel from a drawer, lays it on the table, and pours the warm buttery onions on top. She wraps it up and reaches for my arm.

I pull back quickly. *Are you crazy?*

She shakes her head, reaches again for my elbow.

No one knows where I am.

I jump up.

She makes that soft clucking noise and waits for me to make up my mind. The rain pelts at the window in cold hard little pecks.

"I need your phone."

Swanson points past the bathroom and down the hall. Inside a room smaller than even mine, there's a single wooden bed covered with another quilt, a nightstand topped with so many books there is hardly room enough for a lamp (my papa's nightstand used to look like this), a dresser with a mirror on top, and a braided rug on the floor. The phone sits on a small table under the window.

I wonder why someone who doesn't speak has a phone, but there is an answering machine, and when I lift the receiver, there's a dial tone.

I pause. Harry's going to wring my neck. I wait, listening as my breath follows a path to my toes. I picture my grandpa and what he's going to do and I make another decision. I hang up.

I will find another way.

69

I lift the corner of the tea towel and consider the onions.

The World Book of Unbelievable and Spectacular Things has a whole chapter on healing herbs and it mentions the ancient power of onions. If I can get healed quickly enough, maybe I won't need Harry.

When I let Swanson touch my elbow, she feels around the bones of my arm the way you would check the leg of a horse. Her fingers are callused like my grandpa's. She wraps the onions around my elbow and I am reminded of the sharp peppery smell of hash browns sizzling on a grill.

Swanson's dog gets up carefully and navigates to the window, where the rain is once again pounding against the glass. She whimpers and then pilots herself back across the rug to where we are sitting. Swanson watches her dog anxiously and her heavy glasses are too big for her face and she has to keep sliding them up. Her dog brushes against her over and over, then makes her way back to the window, whining. I wonder what's wrong.

I sip my cocoa and think about what it's like to be a blind dog. How do you do any of the things dogs like to do? How do you chase squirrels (or cats), dig bones, jump up on the bed to snuggle with the one you love?

My thoughts are interrupted as the dog jumps at the back door and bays like a wolf moaning at the moon. Swanson pushes her cocoa mug away and makes that odd clucking noise, but this time the dog doesn't listen. It howls. Finally, Swanson goes over to an old hutch on the other side of the room, opens the top drawer, and pulls out a collar and a red leash (the one with gold stars all over).

My heart explodes.

70

"Where's my dog?" My heart bellows like an old cow and I jump up, not caring about the onions or how they are spilling all over the floor.

Instead of answering, Swanson points to the milk bottles lined up by the back door.

She shakes her head, points to the leash and collar in her hand, then back to the milk bottles.

Her dog whines. I look from the door to the dog to Swanson. My heart is seriously wondering what we are doing still standing here.

Swanson points to the milk bottles again and my toes start their warning thing but I press them hard into the floor until they whimper. The dog noses the milk bottles so they clink against each other. Swanson waits for me to understand what she is trying to tell me.

When I look at her, my brows raised, she pulls a
tattered notebook out of a drawer and in wavy birdlike
handwriting spells out:

Milk truck

It takes several moments for the words to reach my
heart. I feel like I did when my papa brought me to the
ocean and I got tossed under the waves, one after the
other, and salt water pushed up my nose and choked
down my throat and I tumbled over and over and nothing made sense in the churning, crashing, upside-down,
somersaulting world below the sea.

Now I fall into my chair, dazed, turning blue, because I can't get enough air.

All of a sudden I know the terrible thing that's happened to my dog.

71

"Never knew a bigger pain in the neck in my life," the milkman told me. "That dog is going to get me killed."

My Gloaty Gus had a thing about the milkman from the first day he saw the white uniform with the name TONY embroidered on the chest, and I'd have to hold on to my very bad dog until the truck drove off, but then a team of horses couldn't stop Augustus from breaking free and biting at the tires like they were cats.

The milkman used to take bets on how long it would be before Augustus got himself run over, and my papa told him there's something wrong in your head if you can even joke like that in front of a kid.

"Who says I'm joking?"

"Get out!" my papa yelled from behind the counter, and after that we got our milk from Shop Value.

* * *

I have that dizzy feeling I get when I am too high on the fire escape. The letters swim on the page of Swanson's notebook and I slump on the table because my insides can't hold me up anymore.

The old dog whines and hobbles over to me, sniffing at my knees. Swanson frets over my elbow and I let her unroll and reroll the towel with the onions. I have no strength and couldn't push her away if I tried.

She clucks that odd noise as she tucks my arm back against my side. I try to make the pictures in my head stop—my Augustus chasing the milk truck, biting the wheels, the terrible surprise and crushing power of the rubber tires.

I hold the leash against my face with my good arm. It still smells of warm clumpy dog fur.

My heart beats a soft mourning song.

After all this time,
I've really lost him?

Swanson pulls her coat from a peg on the wall, takes her hunting hat off the shelf, and slides it onto her head. She holds a spare coat out for me, but I sit where I am.

My heart careens inside my chest, dashing against

one rib and then another, unsure how to beat properly or even where it belongs.

After all this time,
I've really lost him?

I let the towel slip from my elbow, press my hand on my throbbing brow, try to block the pictures in my head.

Her old dog whines. Swanson writes in her notebook:

I'm sorry, Jack's girl. I'll show you.

I don't want to see the place where I lost my Gloaty Gus. Swanson walks to the door three times and keeps coming back and pulling on my good arm to get me to follow, but I sit where I am.

My head short-circuits, hornets whirl. It's a good thing my mum isn't here. The snorting bull rearing inside me would shove her under the waves.

72

The only reason I let Swanson pull me up is because it's been eons since anyone called me Jack's girl.

Rain falls in thick sheets and we are soaked before we reach the driveway. I hold my elbow close to my chest and the old dog leans her soggy body against Swanson as she plods ahead. This is how we shuffle along, silently. Finally, an adult who doesn't talk all the time.

I am surprised when we turn sharply toward the tractor strung up with the poison ivy. This is a long way for the milk truck to come. But when we reach the apple orchard, where the trees are bent like old men, Swanson points to several small crosses, all made of branches, all without names.

My heart splits. So this is what she meant. She wasn't going to show me where my dog died, she was going to show me where he is buried.

Water streams down my forehead and into my eyes and inside the coat, many sizes too big. Swanson pulls the hood higher on my head. It smells of fireplaces and dogs, maybe a little of Augustus.

Swanson's old dog noses at my side. My legs shake. I lean against one of the apple trees but even that can't hold me up and I slip and land in a lump on the ground and stay there for a very long time, and the tears come then, finally, after all these months, and they come slowly at first and then they are a river let loose, and I sob and sob and sob because the hole in my heart is bigger than even the universe.

13

Swanson grabs my good arm to pull me up but I slump so far into the ground I become part of the earth and I breathe in the wet smell of fallen leaves.

She clucks at her old dog, snapping her fingers, and the dog (that is not my dog) sniffs the air with her white muzzle raised and barks a moaning yelp—which I now know could never be my dog's.

I take a deep hollow aching breath, and when I let it out, Swanson tugs at my coat to get me up.

The ground tilts, the sky wails, the earth moans.

After all this time,
I've lost him.

Swanson's old dog hobbles through the wet grass, sniffing constantly, brushing up against logs and boulders, navigating from one apple tree to the next, pointing her muzzle into the rain, following a compass I cannot see.

She yaps again through all the pouring rain, and again and again and again.

And then, from somewhere deep inside the chicken coop, a rich booming glorious bark reaches out through the hurtling rain to find me.

I jump up.

I'd know that bark anywhere.

After all this time,
I haven't lost him.

Then, still dizzy, with muscles weak as Jell-O and toes that are gushing about how they knew all along that everything would work out, I run. Just like in Harry's old movies, I fly, and when I reach the chicken coop and yank open the door, my Gloaty Gus leaps on me, and of course I fall—because he is such a big lug—and he licks my face like I am a piece of sweet butterscotch and my cheeks are also wet from the rain.

It is all I ever hoped it would be.

74

It takes the rest of the afternoon, but thanks to Swanson's old notebook and a tattered diary she pulls from the nightstand by her bed, I finally piece things together.

Her dog's name is Queenie, although once upon a time it was Emmeline Morning Star of Boston, and my toes breathe a sigh of relief that things got changed. Queenie is a purebred golden retriever and, unlike my mutt Augustus, was given a very formal show name by her former owner.

Queenie never won a single ribbon, though, because she began losing her sight as a puppy and Swanson rescued her right after. She is twelve now and sleeps on Swanson's bed, and when Augustus saw how things were here, he told them *roll over Beethoven*, and I wonder how they all fit, since my Gloaty Gus is such a pillow hog.

Swanson began locking Augustus in the chicken coop and sometimes the barn on milk delivery days because of that thing he has about the milk truck. She padlocked the barn because she was worried about Avery Taylor coming out. She also couldn't leave him in the house because we all know how he jumps out.

He broke two windows.

It all makes sense when you think about it. My mum giving my dog away—that's what doesn't make sense.

Your mother told me you didn't want him anymore. I would never have taken him if I had known.

I pull Augustus up on the couch and wrap the quilt over us, and when he is all snuggled up next to me, he sighs and gets his Gloaty Gus look on him, like he has the best life of any dog ever, and of course I have to hug him because he is right.

We stay like this for a very long time—with the rain pouring down outside and the love of a great dog keeping me warm. Swanson rewraps the onions, and the dog (that is not my dog) pads over and noses into our business, looking at us with her eyes that never open, whining, and then she lies down in front of the couch, dropping her muzzle on the rug.

It is too much for Augustus. Before I can grab him, he jumps on the floor and licks at that spot just above Queenie's nose, then circles until he finds the right place. He flops down and nestles his head in the warm place between her chin and chest.

I call him back to me but he makes that sigh that big dogs make and nestles closer to Queenie and that's the exact moment a worry worm begins winding its way into my heart.

75

Swanson slices a fat loaf of homemade bread, melts butter in an old fry pan, and sprinkles it with cinnamon, nutmeg, and cloves.

She slices a banana and fries the pieces in the spiced butter. She spreads the bread with crunchy peanut butter, lays sizzling banana slices on top, then fries the whole sandwich. When she puts it in front of me, the bread is toasty and buttery.

While I eat the best sandwich of my life, the rain pours against the windows and thumps the roof. Every so often Queenie moans in her sleep and Augustus pricks his ears forward and lifts his head to look at her. He keeps licking that spot just above her nose. I try to pull him back to me, but he snuggles closer to her.

I snap my fingers and call Augustus and he looks

up for a minute, grins that grin, and burrows closer to Queenie. When she tries to get up but can't get a good hold on the floor after lying there for so long, Swanson lifts under her belly. Stone-faced, I watch Augustus yawn, stand up, stretch long and deep, and push his flank against hers so they can navigate the room together.

"Get over here," I snap, but Augustus ignores me as Swanson opens cans of Blue Buffalo dog food. She fills two bowls and sets them on the floor. When Queenie sticks her face in the one on the left, Augustus gently nudges her to the other side.

One good thing, Augustus still eats like a wolf.

76

Swanson wants to show me something.

She pulls two harnesses out of the hutch and straps one on Queenie, and when she buckles Augustus into the other, he sits tall and barrels out his chest.

Then Swanson snaps one end of a rope to Queenie and the other to Augustus, yoking them like sled dogs, like oxen, like beads on a string.

She motions for me to follow her to the porch. Outside in the pouring rain, she makes that clucking noise and waves her hand at Augustus, and he jumps off the porch like a horse rushing out of the gate, and Queenie jumps, too. Harness bells ring through the rain and Augustus slows his pace for just a moment so Queenie can match his powerful stride.

My heart swells as my Gloaty Gus and Queenie fly

through the sopping fields, flanks heaving, tails soaring, fur rippling. Water flies off the tall grass as they jump over logs and gallop toward the apple orchard, heads high, Augustus setting the course, Queenie, with her eyes closed, trusting, her left shoulder brushing against his right.

I hear my mum telling me at least he's making something of himself, and the worry worm plunges to the center of my heart.

After a few minutes Augustus leads Queenie back to the porch, and even though my toes keep warning me that part of Augustus belongs to Queenie now, I heave a tennis ball into the wet field and watch them run side by side, and the tall grass weeps right alongside me.

He is her conductor, her leader, her guide, her friend, and together they fly across the field for the ball. Like a lead sled dog, he has a job to do and a grin on his face. I push my mum's voice out of my head so I can talk to my papa:

What do I do? I can't leave him here with them.

When I get no answer, I tell my papa: *I won't give up the true-blue friend of my soul when I've just found him. I won't. Don't even ask me to do that.*

My papa is silent, as he is more and more these days so I can work things out for myself.

God's bones, I tell him, *I could use some help.*

77

"Are you *insane?*" is what Harry roars when he jumps out of his truck.

I try not to concentrate on the fire that shoots out his eyes.

"I've been looking for you for hours! You could've been killed riding your bike in that hailstorm. You could be *dead in a ditch!*"

Swanson's knuckles go white squeezing the porch column. Her bone face turns ash.

Rain slides off Harry's fishing hat and onto his yellow slicker. Augustus and Queenie trot out to the porch, and the screen door snaps behind them. They have been resting by the woodstove after flying through the sopping fields, and hearing Harry bellow, Queenie sniffs the wet air, then pushes her muzzle into Swanson's knee.

Augustus takes one look at Harry and barks his bloody head off. I grab for his collar but of course he'll have none of that and he leaps off the porch and roars about five feet from Harry's work boots. With the scruffy fur on his back raised up like knight's pikes, he doesn't make a good impression.

Augustus doesn't believe in people yelling at me.

Harry doesn't believe in barking dogs.

It's a terrible combination.

"No, Augustus! Bad dog. Bad, *bad, bad* dog!" I yell, flying off the porch into the pouring rain. I lunge, but Augustus sprints away, circling back to bark at Harry, and already my toes are warning me that things could go very badly for my dog and me if I don't do something quickly.

I leap and my fingers barely touch my dog's wet fur before sliding off. "Augustus, stop that *now!*"

My very bad dog ignores me and dashes around my grandpa's feet, barking and sending fountains of puddle water spurting up.

Harry balls his fists.

Cheetahs claw inside my head. "No, Augustus! Bad dog. Bad, bad, *bad* dog."

When Augustus takes a breath to glance at Queenie, I jump and fly on top of him, belly-flopping, plunging my fingers into his fur, cinching his collar with a choke hold.

My dog whimpers and I feel terrible. I scratch his ears and whisper that he better knock it off.

Smoke is circling Harry's ears when I finally look up.

"I found my dog," I say finally.

"I see that."

Harry looks incredulously at Swanson. "*You've* had her dog all this time?"

Swanson backs up a few paces. Somehow she has managed to get her wool hunting hat pulled down to her nose. Queenie whines and burrows into her leg.

I hear my papa in my head: *Show Harry. Show him what your dog can do.*

I drag my dog to the porch and pull the harnesses off the hook. Augustus barrels out his chest when I link him to Queenie. Then Swanson makes that clucking noise and sweeps her arm, and Augustus jumps off the porch and Queenie follows.

This time they head for the barn. Augustus gently arcs his body around the edges of the building and Queenie glides like a sailing ship beside him. When they come around the back, his chest muscles ripple and there's a grin on his face.

Harry opens his mouth, closes it.

I notice my bike is already in the back of the truck.

My grandpa pulls his hat off and rubs his temples. He sees me looking at my bike.

"I saw it in the bushes. I didn't know where you were. All this rain . . . it's a flood. I'd been looking for hours when finally Philippe told me about that snake in the suitcase and that you were bringing it out here. What I couldn't figure out was *why would you do that?*"

Hornets whirl. I could wring Philippe's neck for telling on me.

I brace myself for more fire, but Harry leaves the snake subject alone. Instead, while my dog flies across the wet fields and through the apple orchard once more, he pulls me close. It is the first time he has hugged me that I can ever remember and the metal clasps on his slicker pinch.

"I told your mother I knew nothing about raising a girl," he whispers in that gruff Marines voice that makes even steering wheels steer straighter. "But I'm not giving you up for anything, Rosie." And then he hugs me so tight I have to make a space so I can breathe.

When my dog finally leads Queenie back to the porch, they flop down together, panting. Swanson unhooks the harnesses.

"How is that even possible?" I can't tell if Harry is talking about Augustus helping Queenie or me finding my dog.

"Let's go home," he says after a while. "Go get your dog."

Harry climbs in the truck and waits for me, tapping his thumbs on the steering wheel. My papa would have gone over and said something kind to Swanson, but Harry is not my papa.

I take a few steps toward the porch. The worry worm plunges deeper and my toes warn me that many things have changed over the past year. My mum would say I lost my potential. I would say my dog found his.

I call to Augustus but he nuzzles closer to Queenie. I call again and again and then I realize in one terrible moment how dashed my dreams really are.

Eventually I turn back in the pouring rain, tears streaming down my face, and climb into the truck. Harry starts the motor, shifts the truck into reverse, puts one arm around me and one on the wheel, waits without words.

My dog sits up and raises his ears and barrels out his chest. Swanson is too far away for me to hear that odd clucking noise, but she waves her arm out in front of her and in one mighty leap my Gloaty Gus jumps off the porch.

I open the truck door and Augustus jumps in.

"Unbelievable," my grandpa says.

78

At a little before six o'clock on Sunday night, Harry grabs his fishing hat and heads for the door.

"Stop!"

Augustus looks up from his spot under the table.

"Why can't *you* talk to her?"

"I don't need to talk to her. You do." Harry picks up the paper bag filled with little flags and pulls a clean apron from the laundry basket by the couch.

"I don't want to talk to her."

He leaves his yellow slicker on the coatrack because finally, after all these days, the rain has stopped. "You're not the sharpest pencil in the box, are you?"

Hornets whirl when my grandpa talks like this. *Cow-flop-breath.*

"You work it out with her, things will go better for you. That's all."

"But she gave my dog away." I can't help the whine that flies out of my mouth.

"People forget how much a kid can love a dog, Rosie."

Well, isn't that the truth. "I don't want her to take me to California."

"Did I ever once say anything about giving you up? Now go ice that elbow."

Fine. I dump ice cubes into a plastic bag and toss one on the floor because ever since he's lived with Swanson, Augustus has a thing about ice cubes.

Harry slams the door and the picture of me, Augustus, and my papa flips on the floor. I pick it up, swipe off the grit. Of the three of us in that picture, only one of us is still missing.

My papa would understand how I don't want to talk to the person who gave the true-blue friend of my soul away, and why do I have to? When the phone rings, I let it go until it stops. A few minutes later it rings again.

My dog and I decide to take a nap. I pull the army blanket over our heads. The Old Spice smell is long gone and in its place is the warm clumpy smell of dog fur.

I snuggle up to him and doze off. When the phone rings a third time, my toes start their warning thing that maybe Harry is right.

"Rosalita?"

"It's Rosie."

My mum pauses. "Yes." She stops, takes a breath.

"I called to remind you that I will arrive in a little over a week."

I scratch that long skinny spot at the top of my dog's nose. I can hear my mum's breathing.

"Did you hear me, Ro?"

I nod. *Ro?*

The early-evening train rumbles into town. Our whole apartment building shakes and grit sifts through the screens.

My mum breathes sharply, then sighs, softening her voice. "I want you to think more before I arrive about my idea of moving you out here. We have wonderful schools in California"

"I found my dog," I snap, sinking my nose deeper into his clumpy dog fur.

My mum is quiet; I hear her breathing. "Your grandfather told me. He cussed me out, as you can imagine."

I didn't know that. Augustus makes that deep sigh that big dogs make.

"I'm fine here." I scratch my Gloaty Gus on his chest the way he likes.

"Yes, I understand that. But you almost had to repeat the entire last school year. You must admit that you're not much of a success with your grandfather. But if you came out here, you could have a fresh start, really begin making something of yourself."

I breathe in sharply. Augustus flicks his ears.

"Did you hear me, Ro?"

The train whooshes to a stop and passengers get off and their voices drift through my window screen.

"This is so frustrating." My mum inhales deeply, then breathes out one-two-three. She relaxes her voice. "I want to tell you something."

My toes brace themselves. I reach for Augustus.

"My mother—you never met her, but she did nothing with her life. Nothing. She cleaned 7-Elevens. That was her job, a whole string of 7-Elevens, one after the other, six days a week. On Sundays she slept. I wanted more for my life, and I want more for you. What I don't understand is why don't you want it, too?"

I wonder what she thinks of me sweeping the donut shop, scrubbing all the glass, wiping crumbs off the counters a million times a day.

I feel the irritated huffs in my mum's breathing. There's a long pause before she says, "I could fight for custody if I wanted, and unlike your grandfather, I could afford a long battle. But what I really want is for *you* to *want* to come."

There's a blank space in my throat where words used to be. I hear my papa in my head: *Harry came looking for you how many times now?*

I dive further under the army blanket. "I'm not leaving my dog."

My mum's disappointment in me rushes through the wire.

"I have some brochures for boarding schools that I want to look at together." My mum pauses. Then: "A school like that could help you become anything you want to be."

I wonder if you can bring dogs to boarding school. I decide that you can't. And my papa says, *What about Harry?*

After a minute, I whisper, "I'm fine here."

Her only reply is a quick impatient burst of breath that races through the phone, then she hangs up.

79

The thing about my Augustus is that when he wants to be patted, too bad for you if you don't feel like it.

He shoves his nose into my side, tickling me. He licks the donut jelly stuck between my fingers. When I push him away, he pokes at my smashed elbow and pulls at the new bandage from the doctor's office.

"Stop that!" I am irritated that his dog drool is the reason Harry is making me wash all the shopwindows on a day when I can only use one arm and the sun is so hot that steam hisses off the sidewalk.

I push my very bad dog away but he comes back for more, and this time he steals the cleaning cloth and runs off down Main Street, dangling it between his teeth.

I toss the bottle of Windex and chase after him just as Mr. Peterson rides down the hill on his bike, his twins hollering and waving cherry-red Popsicles from the bright orange cart bolted to the back. Balloons flap off the rear reflector light.

I hear my papa in my head: *This isn't good.*

Eddie the Barber is just leaving the donut shop when Mr. Peterson shoots by—his youngest one in a baby backpack, fat little dumpling legs hanging down, pea-sized toes wiggling.

Mr. Peterson flies over the biggest pothole and the back wheel wobbles and the cart tips and Mr. Peterson has to stop and that's when Augustus drops the cleaning cloth and gallops over. The twins shriek as my very bad dog jumps in and tries to find a spot for his moose rear.

"No, Augustus! Bad dog. Bad, bad, *bad* dog."

My very bad dog licks the twins' Popsicles and waits for the patting of his life. I grab his collar and pull. Mr. Peterson pushes, but we can't get past the thumping tail.

"Augustus, *get off.*"

Already the balloons are soaring for the sky but the twins haven't noticed because they are hugging Augustus. Then the baby howls from the backpack and Mr. Peterson looks around for the binky but Augustus has seen it first and dives for it.

"*Bad dog!*" I pry his mouth open—because my Gloaty Gus would never give up a prize so wonderful as a baby-licked binky on his own—and then I wipe the dog goo off on my shirt and give it back to Mr. Peterson. He looks at it, at the baby wailing, then wipes the pacifier on his shirt and pushes it into the baby's mouth.

"I can fix this," I blurt out, trying to grab my dog's collar, but he is much more interested in the Popsicle sticks. The cart is twisted at a funny angle on the ground. The wheels spin. More than anything I want to get out of this mess before Harry sees.

80

Of course, as we wheel Mr. Peterson's bike and cart up the driveway, Cynthia has to come right over. Her lips glisten from grape soda.

"Go away," I snap.

"Wow, I never had a teacher come to my house before. Are you going to tutor all of us, Mr. Peterson? I really want to be in your class, can I when I'm old enough? I know Philippe is going to your class, but Rosie didn't get good grades."

My blood boils. "Get your nose out of my business, Cynthia."

Mr. Peterson frowns and turns to Philippe. "I'm looking forward to having you in my class this year. Your cartography skills will be a big help to me when we begin our Age of Exploration unit."

I don't even know what *cartography* means. I also don't know why Philippe gets to go to his class and I don't. I roll my eyes.

When Mr. Peterson steps away to change the baby's diaper and Augustus follows him, all interested in the smell, I let Philippe have it: "I told you not to tell Harry about the snake! You could have gotten me in so much trouble."

"Shut up, Rosie. Your grandfather was *really* worried and you don't have to be so mean to everyone." There are spikes in Philippe's voice, tall as skyscrapers. His coat is unbuttoned all the way down to his high-tops and this fires me up even more because he never used to do that with me. Blood pounds through my ears. I crush his bones with my eyes.

"I don't need *you* to tell me how to be nice to Harry." My toes warn me about going too far, but I see Philippe not bothered at all about the nest in Cynthia's hair or about how she scratches and how they don't even *ask* me to do things with them anymore (not that I would say yes anyway) and I stomp further into the angry ocean churning all around me: "I bet if you had a decent mother, Philippe, she'd think you were so horrible she'd pretend she didn't know you."

He gulps and turns radish red. Cynthia's eyes pop. "Oh yeah, Rosie? How come you're here, anyway? I thought they locked the zoo so you couldn't get out."

I ball my fists until they are the size of watermelons.

"I didn't know you were friends," Mr. Peterson says, all of a sudden back beside us with a stinking diaper in his hands and Augustus on his heels.

"We're not," Philippe mutters. He pulls Cynthia's shirt. "Come on."

Philippe's coat hangs so far off his shoulders that it's not much more than a loose cape. My toes whisper something ridiculous like isn't it nice that he doesn't have to button up so far anymore, but I ignore them.

"You don't let kids wear stupid coats like that in your class, do you, *Mr. Peterson*?" The twins hear the lasso-whipping snap in my voice and stop scruffing my dog's fur. Philippe sinks into his coat and now Cynthia pulls at him, saying, "Come on, you don't have to listen to her."

Mr. Peterson raises both brows. "In my class, Rosie, you can wear mittens on your ears if you want."

I seethe. The stink of dirty diaper soars up my nose and there's a bad taste in my mouth. Mr. Peterson sends the twins to the worm pile to dig with Augustus and I get Harry's toolbox. The wheel is pretty easy to straighten with a few quick (one-armed) turns of the wrench.

The problem is the nut that holds the tow bar to

the bike. I get it to twist a quarter of a turn before my wrench slips off.

"Your mother called."

I can't help the screech that flies out of my mouth.

"She asked for the principal, but unfortunately I was the only one around."

I squeeze the wrench and twist. Sparks fly.

"She thinks you're not making much of yourself. I agreed with her, at least as far as school goes."

Augustus lets the twins rub dirt in his fur. He rolls over so they will rub his belly. I grit my teeth, use both my arms, and twist harder. My head throbs. I could use an ice cube.

I get the wrench to turn a bit more.

"She wants me to move to California." I twist so hard the wrench nearly melts.

"You don't want to go?"

"I can't bring my dog to boarding school," I snort.

The wrench slips. Fire shoots out my ears. Mr. Peterson takes the screwdriver and wrench but his fingers are too thick to reach the tight space.

I try again. I give the wrench steady pressure and begin to twist only after I count to five. This time it works.

When we finally get the cart hooked on right, Mr. Peterson loads his twins back in, snuggles the baby into the backpack, and climbs onto the bike.

"I told your mother you're no fool, Rosie. Your grandfather tells everyone who comes in the donut shop how you got your dog back—and now the whole town is talking about it. "I'd say a kid like that can do just about anything she puts her mind to, wouldn't you?"

81

The next morning Augustus sulks.

"Stop that."

He buries his soft muzzle under the army blanket. Every so often he makes that sigh that big dogs make and gets up, circles to find a better spot, and flops back down.

Later he turns his nose up at his kibble. The train roars through town and he drinks a little water from the toilet bowl, then jumps back on my bed. I check his eyes, scratch him between the ears, and sneak him some of Harry's sardines, which he gobbles in one bite.

"You live *here* now," I snap.

Harry comes home for lunch and sees my dog is acting like a flat tire. He reaches in the refrigerator for his sardines, notices they are nearly gone, and tosses the can on the table.

"You might as well give him the rest." He opens another can and toasts rye bread and makes a sardine and onion sandwich. "I told Mrs. Salvatore I would build a raft for that boy," he says between bites. "I could use some help."

I roll my eyes.

Of course Cynthia wants to go build a raft, too, and Harry says she can come if she keeps her big trap shut. When she sees me, she asks Harry why aren't I going? Harry ignores her and tells Philippe, "You can't build a raft with a coat on. Take it off."

I open my window, wedge myself through the skinny space, and climb onto the fire escape. The iron ladder sways as the wind gusts down from the sandpits.

My dog is uninterested. He snoozes under the army blanket.

I go in and hook his leash on and make him come out. He whines the whole time. I frown and tell him, "You're not going to amount to much if you don't put a little effort in."

Another train roars into town, shaking the apartment building, sending grit up my nose. Passengers get off and more get on and the train rumbles away. Soon it will pass the far fields at Swanson's, where I know Queenie is waiting.

The truth is this: now that my dog has a job to do, he *is* making something of himself.

"Oh, all right," I snort. *"All right!"*

82

When I finally get the Blackbird's wheel straight and the chain back on, Augustus practically pulls me up Main Street, which is pretty fun if you think about it.

Swanson seems to know we are coming, because Queenie already has her harness on.

I hold Augustus and unhook his red leash (the one with gold stars all over) and he flies for Queenie. They spend many minutes sniffing each other and then Augustus licks her nose and she licks the clumpy fur behind his ears.

I think about making her stop because I just used the no-tangle spray Harry bought at Walmart, but Augustus is thumping his tail and he has that grin on his face that used to be reserved for only me and now I have to share it.

"Augustus misses her."

Swanson nods, a smile in her eyes.

"I think he's happier here, but I don't want him to be." I let a little moan escape from the bottom of my heart.

After a few minutes of watching them, Swanson motions for me to come inside and she pours me a glass of lemonade. My eyes fill but I gnaw at the inside of my cheek until they stop.

Swanson's little notebook is already on the table. She writes:

Your dog needs YOU!

She underlines the last part and waits for me to say more.

The good thing about Swanson is she doesn't hog the discussion. She nods and listens and every so often pats my hand but mostly she looks straight at me and waits for me to get to the next sentence. And I suddenly have a lot to say: about Augustus wanting to be with Queenie so much, about my mum wanting to move me to California, about living with Harry, about Philippe and his coat, and about Cynthia being such a pest. I even tell her about my papa and how Harry wants me to visit and how I don't think it's a very good idea.

Not many people have a listening ear like my papa, but Swanson does. It helps if you don't talk much, but it's more than that—the difference is you listen with your heart open and you are not thinking the whole time about what you are going to say next. It's not about trying to figure out your next move, like you do in Monopoly. It's about love. I decide I might try this with Augustus.

He looks up from where he is lying next to Queenie and he looks at me with those gooseberry eyes and this time I know what *he* is feeling.

83

When I get all the words out, Swanson fries me a peanut butter sandwich.

I lick the melted peanut butter dripping off my little finger and watch Augustus and Queenie flop on the floor.

"How did you teach a blind dog to do so much?"

Swanson pulls out her notebook and writes a few sentences. Then she makes that chicken cluck and calls Queenie over. She shows me how she guides Queenie through the house, every day, never taking a day off, showing her the hot stove, the sharp edges of the table, the steep cellar stairs, the coffee table, the tall lamp, the couch, the grandfather clock.

It is the same outdoors. Swanson walks Queenie out through the apple orchard every day, carefully passing by big boulders and fallen logs, letting Queenie stop to sniff everything, which, if you've ever had a dog before, you know can take a thousand years.

Eventually Queenie learned where the trees were in the apple orchard and how to find the barn and the chicken coop on her own. She learned she could chase squirrels—barking happily—if she knew where the trees were so she didn't plow into them.

When Augustus moved in, Swanson yoked the dogs together while she showed Queenie—over and over—where the danger spots were. Each day she made the course more difficult and finally she took both dogs across town to the sandpits after working hours.

Now Swanson's eyes fill. She bends over her notebook and writes:

I was surprised the day I let go of the leash and they continued on without me.

84

We are interrupted by a car screeching outside. Augustus roars.

I fly to the window in time to see Avery Taylor running up the driveway with a bucket in his hand. His friends yell and hoot as he throws fire-engine-red paint at Swanson's jeep.

Augustus leaps at the window and then Avery Taylor climbs back into his Camaro and revs his engine and peels out, screeching his tires like they are cats.

Augustus knocks out the window screen.

"No, Augustus! Bad dog. Bad, bad, *bad* dog!" I yell, grabbing his collar, pulling him back inside. He wriggles out of my grasp and lunges for the window.

In one jump Swanson pulls him and makes her

chicken-clucking noise and snaps her fingers, and Augustus sits.

He whines, looking mournfully at me, but he keeps his big moose rear on the floor, where Swanson says it belongs.

Huummmppff, I think.

85

"Why don't you tell the police?"

The noise that comes out of Swanson's throat sounds something like she thinks I am an idiot.

Her eyes are incredulous. She grabs her notebook from the counter and bears down hard.

NO!

I push the notebook right back.

"Why?"

We are interrupted by Augustus, who, after investigating the jeep and the new paint splashed all over, wants to come back inside. Queenie has red paint on her nose.

Swanson wipes Queenie's nose with Joy dish soap.

I wait for a hundred years for her to answer my question. When she doesn't, I switch to the other thing I am thinking about.

"Why don't you talk, *ever?*"

Swanson tries to distract me with another sandwich but I say no, sit back down, I know what she is up to. Augustus follows the tone of my voice like a bouncing ball and watches me from his spot on the rug. I tell him to mind his business.

"Everybody gets you wrong. So why don't you give them a chance to know you?"

God's bones, she motions for me to go home.

I tell her no, I am not going. I stand my ground. "Kids are afraid of you, don't you know that?" I hand her the notebook. I tell her I am not leaving without an answer. I am serious about this.

Augustus is all interested in the situation. He stands up, stretches his long legs, and comes over by me. I scratch behind his ears the way he likes.

I push the notebook closer.

Swanson stares out the window for what seems like a day and a half.

I push the notebook even closer, pick up the pencil, hold it out.

When she takes it, she sits down and very slowly begins to write:

I haven't talked since I was eight.

I wait for her to write more, but she sits there.

Gently I prod her: "And that was it? You never talked after that?"

She shrugs.

"Not even in school? Don't you get lonely? Don't you want friends?"

I think about Cynthia saying I am a terrible friend, and who would want a friend like me, and I'm not sure I want friends, but sometimes I do. Life is very confusing.

After a while, I ask, "Well, do you have any black paint?"

86

Philippe rolls a three and lands on Baltic and buys it. I laugh at him because has there ever been a more worthless piece of property?

I decide to try a new tactic and not buy anything until I get to Park Place.

I shoot two threes, land on Oriental, and roll again.

"Hey, wait a minute, you're not going to buy that?" Philippe leans forward.

"No, it's junk." I shake the dice.

"I'll buy it, then."

"You can't do that."

"Of course I can. I'll buy it for a dollar."

"What? You can't." I sit forward. My springy curls fall in my face and I push them away. "I don't want *you* to have it."

"Too bad. The rules say if you don't buy something, I can make an offer." He talks very slowly, like I am a dunce. "And since Cynthia won't want it, I can take it for a dollar." He pulls a Monopoly dollar out.

"He's right," Cynthia says. "It's really something that you don't know this, Rosie."

God's bones, she is infuriating. It is nearly a hundred degrees and way too hot to ride out to Swanson's, which is why I am playing Monopoly, trying to work my way into the conversation I want to have with Philippe.

My dog is bored to death. If Harry hadn't started buying soup bones to keep Augustus busy, he'd be sitting on top of the Monopoly board, his tail thumping. Instead, he's flopped in the corner, chomping loudly.

A fly buzzes at the window screen, trying to reach the bone.

I grab the rule book and flip through. This bores me in about thirty seconds. I roll the dice again, land on Electric Company. What I really want is Boardwalk and Park Place—or if not that, at least the railroads.

While Philippe is buying everything he lands on, Cynthia picks at her scab. I sneak a hundred-dollar bill from the bank and then two fifties.

Philippe lands on Marvin Gardens. I slip another hundred under my knee and then one more. Stealing makes the game less gouge-your-eyes-out boring.

Philippe moves to Pacific Avenue. I land on Atlantic and hand the dice back to Philippe.

"Aren't you going to buy anything?" he asks. His coat is off.

"I'm waiting for Boardwalk."

"You can't win with Boardwalk because no one ever lands on it and you will spend all your money for nothing. You would be much better off if you watched how I play and did that."

I ignore him. I roll the dice. Bam, I am on Park Place.

Then I get another speech on how I should start small with St. Charles Place and how I should especially try to buy all the railroads. "Even the utilities have their purpose, so buy them."

Hornets whir.

I rub my hands together so hard they sizzle. I throw the dice. I land on Boardwalk.

"See?" I roar.

"Hey, is she cheating?" Cynthia asks.

"No, I am not, but we might as well quit right now because I have already won."

Augustus looks up when he hears the spikes in my voice.

Then my dog whines—and it is a good reminder to hold my tongue because I have something I need to do and I need a friend to help me.

I consider if Philippe is my friend anymore or not.

The sun glints like foil. Philippe turns to me, his eyes a hot steely blue.

"Put all the money back, Rosie." His voice is a low sharp arrow that scrapes at the nerves running up the center of my back. "All the money you stole from the bank—every bit of it."

My mouth hangs open; Cynthia rocks on her heels. "I knew she was cheating. I didn't see her but I just knew. This is why you don't have any friends, Rosie. You should look in the mirror and mend your ways. That's what my mama says and she knows a lot of things."

"Shut up, Cynthia."

I pull the money out from under my leg and hand it to Philippe.

"I was just testing you."

He rolls his eyes.

I bide my time and keep quiet as we go around the board a few million more times and Philippe has to buy a trillion houses and even some hotels. "I have something I need to do tomorrow and I was wondering if you would help."

"I can help," Cynthia says, hopping up on her knees. "I like to do things."

Thunder rolls through my face. *For the thousandth time, Cynthia, mind your business.*

I turn back to Philippe. "Yes or no?"

He shrugs.

Hornets whirl. I compose my face and pull all the parts that are tight with fury back into position. I stand up. "I was just going to help someone who means a lot to me, but fine, I'll do it myself."

I grab the leash and together me and my Gloaty Gus stomp out of the room.

Behind me, I hear Cynthia saying to Philippe, "But I like to help people—how come you don't want to do that?"

PART IV

87

I need Swanson to take Augustus, so here's how I do it.

I dial her phone, and when her answering machine picks up and talks in a computer voice, I say: "Can you bring Augustus to your house for the morning? I have something I need to do." Then I hang up.

A few minutes later she drives up in her jeep with Queenie in the front. With all the black paint we spread over the yellow and fire-engine-red splotches, it looks almost new. Augustus jumps right in and Swanson gives him the patting of his life, which I am mostly okay with now that I know he is making something of himself.

I don't tell Swanson about my plan because she would try to stop me.

I don't tell Augustus because he would want to come.

I don't tell Harry because he would say I have the sense of a turnip.

I stuff my message to Avery Taylor deep in my pocket and climb onto the Blackbird.

88

"You ready?" I whisper as the smell of rotten meat soaks into our skin.

"I don't know about this, Rosie." Phillippe lets out a little whine. "What if somebody sees us?"

"We're hiding between dumpsters," I snap, sitting back on my heels. "No one's going to know we're even here."

The heat rises off his coat, and an edge of moldy bread sticks to the bottom of my shoe. I try to rein in my temper.

The Shop Value parking lot is empty this early in the morning. We are waiting for Avery Taylor to start his shift, bagging groceries. He always parks his Camaro in the same spot (by the entrance sign) and he leaves his roof down so everyone can admire his shiny leather seats and polished steering wheel.

Philippe looks at his watch, loosens his helmet. "I just don't want to do this, Rosie."

"But you promised. I already said if you do this, I will play three-player again. Friends do things for each other."

"Well, maybe friends don't ask things like this."

"Just be quiet," I hiss, already hopping mad. "This town loves hockey more than donuts. No one else is going to do anything about Avery Taylor. It's the right thing to do."

Philippe's nerves would make anyone unsteady. I shift my weight so my left hip takes more of the load. My heels dig in the sand.

"But what if he tells the police or something?"

"He won't. They'd ask around why someone would want to do something like this to him and sooner or later they would figure out he is the one doing all these bad things to Swanson." Philippe is *really* getting my goat now and I lash out. "Philippe, your job is the *easy job*." I blow my breath out in a loud angry whoosh.

"All right, all right, you don't have to get mad all the time," he says. "I'll do it."

I pull Harry's work gloves on and remind myself to bury them when I am done.

89

When I open the dumpster, the smell of rotting meat soars up.

Philippe plugs his nose and rolls around on the ground, gagging deep inside his gigantic coat.

"Stop being such a baby," I snort. "You're only the lookout. I'm the one who actually has to do this."

I poke around until I find a pound of hamburger with most of the plastic wrapping off. Already there are maggots crawling around and one gets on my glove. I hold my breath.

The World Book of Unbelievable and Spectacular Things has plenty to say about maggots and how many days it takes for them to start wiggling on a piece of rotten meat. This tells me this hamburger has sweltered in the dumpster for at least twenty-four hours. Three more days and we'll have flies.

Retching, I dump the meat in the trash bag and reach back in for a package of pork chops.

"What are you doing?" Cynthia has snuck up on us and is watching me pull the plastic wrapping off.

I glare at Philippe.

"Nothing. Go away, Cynthia." I drop the chops in the bag.

She plugs her nose. Her eyes are very big. I see how her hair is combed to one side and there is the nest underneath.

"She's going to tell," Philippe groans.

I have to hold my breath so I don't ignite.

"I am not going to tell. Tell about what?"

"Cynthia, you can't be here."

"But why? I want us to start being friends."

"I'll think about it, Cynthia. If you go away." I fish around in the dumpster and pull out a pound of sausage links, already blue.

"But I just want to be your friend."

"Well, you can't, not *now*. I'm busy." I hold the trash bag open and dump in the sausages, and the horrid smell leaks out. "I'll play Ping-Pong and three-player Monopoly and whatever you want later. I just can't do it now. Okay?"

"Even Barbies?"

I boil over. "No, not Barbies. I will never play Barbies. Now leave."

We lose many valuable minutes watching Cynthia sniffle and then finally she runs home. Every couple of seconds, though, she turns back to see if she can see anything or if we have changed our minds.

"If you look back again, I will never play with you!" I scream.

This may not be the smartest thing because a lady pushing a baby carriage stops when she hears the ruckus and we have to hide between the dumpsters—holding the trash bag close—until she walks away.

I feel woozy from the smell. I wonder if you can die from this.

When Avery Taylor drives in, he parks exactly where I thought he would. He spits on his thumb and polishes the door handle. He leaves the top down and walks into the market.

"Okay, now it's your turn," I tell Philippe.

You don't have to tell him twice. He jumps on his red bike, eager to get away from the smell, and pedals into the lot. His job is to ride around, and if anyone comes while I am doing my part, he will fall and pretend he has skinned his knee.

The distraction is the thing.

90

I hold the bag as far from my nose as possible and rush over to Avery Taylor's convertible. The leather seats shine, the steering wheel gleams. He must spend hours on this car. I hear my papa's voice asking me if I am sure I want to do this. I tell him it may not be what he would do or what Harry would do and it sure wouldn't be what Mrs. Salvatore would do, but it is what I would do.

I lift the bag and dump the rotten meat all over the front seats. I use my gloves to spread it out, making sure it is well arranged in a single layer so it will sizzle and stick to the leather. There are maggots everywhere.

When I am done, I race to the dumpsters and pull the Blackbird out of its hiding place. Philippe pedals over, huffing badly under his coat.

"But what if he drives it and the smell gets to him and he passes out and crashes and gets killed? It will be our fault."

"Don't be silly, Philippe. You don't get in an accident because of rotten meat. You don't even *drive* with rotten meat in the car."

Philippe and I pedal out of the parking lot as fast as we can and it isn't until our tires are crackling across the grit on Main Street that I feel the crunching in my back pocket.

I drag my feet to stop, bellowing as loud as Harry: "I forgot the note, Philippe! I forgot to leave the note." Cars zip past, then the milk truck. "I have to go back."

"You can't go back now," Philippe snaps. "Look, there's somebody watching the car."

Sure enough, a man who looks an awful lot like Mr. Peterson is inspecting Avery Taylor's car.

"But this will all be for nothing if I don't leave the note."

I ignore the doubts climbing inside me and turn around. "Somebody has to stick up for Swanson and it won't work if Avery Taylor doesn't read the note. It's the right thing to do, Philippe, you know it is."

I have to wait for the man to leave the car and hurry into the store, and sure enough, he has a baby backpack.

God's bones. I figure I have exactly one minute before Avery Taylor runs out of the store screaming.

I rush back into the parking lot, pedaling as fast as I can, bouncing in a pothole and running over a piece of the plastic meat wrap. I jump off the Blackbird and stick the note to the steering wheel:

> You will never get a hockey scholarship if you bother Swanson again—because we will tell the world how horrible you really are.

I don't have time to admire my work. I turn the Blackbird around and fly it faster than it has ever flown before.

91

Augustus and I sit on the front step watching the sand swirl on the street like sugar.

Wind gusts down from the sandpits, tearing leaves from their branches, sending grit up my nose.

Eddie the Barber has a long line waiting. He holds up a box of dog bones for me to see and sets it right beside the bowl of M&M's. He is good that way.

A taxi drives up, its tires scratching at the sand. I know without looking who is inside.

A thin woman gets out, pays the driver, and pulls out a suitcase and a leather briefcase. She turns and stares at Augustus and me. She has slate-colored eyes, springy curls tucked tight in her ponytail, and a frown bigger than Alaska as she tries to keep her heels out of the grit on the road. I have already given Augustus the talking-to of his life about no jumping.

My mum waves a slow sort of half wave, like she is Queen Elizabeth and knows exactly the way manners work. There are no hugs—just us standing a few feet from each other, me wondering what should happen next.

A leaf from the maple tree twirls across the yard. I straighten my back and hold out my hand. I make it strong, not like a wet trout at all. I wait for her to bend down to pat Augustus, who right now is sitting still as King Tut, but she ignores him (not a good idea) and marches up the steps, leaving the suitcase for me.

Of course, Cynthia is on the steps, her eyes very big. My ears twist.

"Wow, is this your mama, Rosie? I never met your mama before, but I know it's her because she looks just like you. Wow, *exactly*. I didn't even know you had a mama." She holds out her hand, and there is a grape soda stain on her cheek. "Pleased to meet you, ma'am."

I try to push around, not really wanting my mum to see the girl who doesn't brush her hair being friends with me.

Cynthia reaches out and tries to help carry the briefcase. "I bet my mama would invite you up for coffee, ma'am, if she was home, but she's at work, did you know she got a new job at Charlie's Place out on Route 54, Rosie?"

My teeth open enough for a hiss: "Stay out of my business, Cynthia."

But then of course Philippe rushes out of his apartment yelling (in a new happy voice that, come to think of it, I haven't heard before) about how if Cynthia wants to go canning she better hurry up. He is dragging a big trash bag stuffed with empty cans behind him. His gigantic wool coat is unbuttoned to the ground.

He stops short when he sees us. My mum's eyes widen. Augustus thumps his tail. Dog books say you should be ready for bad behavior before it happens, that's the secret to everything, so I wrap the leash around my hand a few more times and reach for our door. I stab the key in our lock because I can't get inside our skinny apartment fast enough.

Inside, the coffeepot is gurgling and Harry has put a plate of jelly donuts on the table.

"Deborah," says my grandpa, pointing to a chair at the table.

"Harry," she says.

And that's pretty much when my very bad dog decides enough is enough with my mum not paying any attention to him while he is still being quiet as King Tut. He takes a flying leap so he stands almost as tall as she is, and when she squeals and pushes him away, he slips and scratches her leg.

"No, Augustus! Bad dog. Bad, bad, *bad* dog."

His tail thumps as he waits for the patting of his life, which doesn't come because my mum loses her balance and grabs the table just in time.

"I'm sorry, I'm sorry." I pull Augustus away and push his big moose rump on the floor. "Bad dog," I say, even though you're not supposed to say that when he is doing something good (which he is now). Then my dog wiggles out of my hands to jump on my mum again. "Augustus, *get off*."

This time Harry stomps on the leash and Augustus sits. *"What are you thinking?"* he roars, and I don't know if he means me or my dog.

Immediately my dog's grin disappears and his eyes grow large and miserable and he crawls under the table. Harry can have that effect on someone.

"You've spent more than a year looking for a dog that is *this* misbehaved? I just don't see the point, Rosalita."

Harry hands my mum a kitchen towel so she can wipe the grit off her leg and he goes to get the Mercurochrome tincture, which she rolls her eyes at. He puts coffee cups on the table, cream and sugar, and little plates and spoons. When he takes a donut, he tears off half and sneaks it to Augustus.

As we sit around eating, my mum reaches in her purse and pulls out some glossy brochures.

"Don't even bother, Deborah." Harry gives Augustus another piece of donut.

"I'm offering her a golden ticket, one that you could never give her."

Harry balls his fist, takes a big slug of coffee. His ears twitch. I see him counting to a million.

"I know you are trying your best," my mum continues, "and of course you live close to her father, but she doesn't even visit him."

Harry gets up to pour more coffee. He grabs a tin of sardines, sneaks a fillet to Augustus, and plops one into his mouth. Then he says, "What's different, Deborah? You've never wanted to be in her life before. Not really."

My mum breathes in sharply. She turns up her nose at the fish smell. "People change."

"Yes, they do," my grandpa says in that gruff Marines voice that makes even the silverware march. "And that's why you should see that Rosie needs to make this decision herself. Too much has happened without her say."

Well, isn't that the truth. I reach down and scratch Augustus between the ears. He thumps his tail and the floor hums. "I'm fine here."

"Yes, I understand that, Rosalita, but what about college? It's never too early to begin making something of yourself." I watch my mum's frustration spread like fog.

Harry eats another sardine and another. "If you'd

open your eyes, Deborah, you'd see Rosie *is* already making something of herself."

I open my mouth, shut it. *I am?*

My papa says in my head: *You are.*

My mum says, "Don't be ridiculous."

I say, "Me and my Gloaty Gus are staying here."

92

While my mum tries to think of the next thing to say, Augustus jumps half on my lap. I scratch him between the ears and realize I know something my mum doesn't: life is better when you love a dog.

"This is so frustrating, Rosalita. I just want to be part of your life."

Harry crushes the sardine tin in his hands. "You can, Deborah. I won't stop you, as long as that's what Rosie wants. She can visit you in California . . . as long as you'll invite her dog, too." I see the grin in Harry's eyes. "Or you can come here as often as you want. But for Pete's sake, she wants to be called Rosie."

I snort. Augustus thumps his tail. The train rumbles into town and shakes our building. Harry whittles the calluses off his thumb. He told me he wants to talk to my mum about finances—"get her to be a little more generous without going to court"—and since Harry can make even the newspapers refold themselves with straight creases, I know this is a real possibility.

Harry pours another cup of coffee and this seems a good time to leave them. When my grandpa gets started, my mum won't know what hit her, which, considering she is the one who left my papa and me for greener pastures all those years ago, she probably deserves.

I open my window and climb out onto the fire escape, and this time Augustus jumps out without me making him.

I hear Mrs. Salvatore yelling next door—"Philippe, stop that roughhousing!"—and I can't help but grin that he's getting yelled at because it means he's found a real place for himself in that family, which is a nice change, considering what he's been through. Then Paulie is yelping and Francesca is howling and Sarah is screaming will everybody be quiet so she can just read her book and then Mrs. Salvatore is shushing everybody and saying what in God's name did she ever do to deserve this, and I know they are getting loved over there. I can hear it through the walls.

Augustus sniffs deeply into my shirt. The last time I wore it I was at Swanson's. I scratch his ears. I've been thinking about something, and maybe it's time to tell him.

I say, "You could go to Swanson's during the day while I'm at school. That way you can help Queenie and come home with me in the afternoon. It would be like sharing."

A sand truck roars by. Augustus makes that sigh that big dogs make. I sink my nose into his warm clumpy dog fur and he snuggles up to me. After a few minutes I tell him, "Stay here."

I climb in my window and get the black-and-white-speckled notebook and crawl back out again. I read the throw-up page that Mr. Peterson wrote. I think about all that's happened to me.

I smell a cake baking in Mrs. Salvatore's kitchen—chocolate, maybe with cherries. I think maybe heaven must smell like that—yum.

I take a deep breath, pick up my pen, and begin:

I, Rosie Gillespie, am unsinkable.
Here's how I got that way.

Augustus looks up and tries to sniff the page.
"Mind your business," I tell him.

93

Harry does not believe in Heinz ketchup.

He thinks the cheap kind from Walmart is good enough.

"This doesn't taste anything like Heinz." I whine because I can do that with Harry now.

"You need to get your head examined," he snaps. "Ketchup's ketchup."

I know that it's not. I glare at him as he pounds the bottom of the bottle with his fist and covers his scrambled eggs with a sweet sticky puddle. By the time he finishes, there is only a dime-sized spot inside the bottle for me.

God's bones, I snort.

"Oh, give me that." He grabs the bottle and stomps to the sink, turning on the faucet and streaming water into the bottle. Then he snaps the cover, shakes, and hands it back to me.

"I'm not eating that! *It's tomato soup.*"

Smoke spurts out his ears. You can tell he is trying to stop the loose cannon inside him. "If it's that important to you," he growls, "we'll get more on the way."

Augustus whines from his spot under the table. I hold my fork midair.

"Where are we going?"

"For a drive."

I consider this. My toes tap a slow warning.

"I already told you I'm never going back to where my papa is." I am serious about this.

"Did I say anything about that? Now get your dog."

Augustus hits his head when we bounce over a pothole and then we speed past St. Camillus and turn onto the road leading to the sandpits.

I run through my head all the places we could be going. Just this morning, when he caught Augustus drinking from the toilet bowl, Harry said, "This dog is a huge pain in the butt," then, not half an hour later, he roared, "There's dog fur all over. Clean it up. And he got into the dog food again. I already told you to keep that pantry door locked."

I glare at my grandpa, even though we are far away

from Swanson's. "I'm not giving my dog back, if that's what you're thinking."

"Stop talking," my grandpa says.

He turns out onto Route 54 and we zip past Charlie's Place, where Cynthia's mama works. I let Augustus crawl over me so he can stick his nose out the window. We pass the high school, the hockey rink, and a furniture store. About a mile later he pulls into a strip mall with a Dairy Queen, a tile and carpeting outlet, and a bicycle repair shop.

"I thought it might be time we fixed that bike, that's all." Harry climbs out of the truck and pulls the Blackbird out from where he has hidden it under a tarp.

My mouth is hanging open, I can tell you that.

I try to keep my dignity.

I am not very successful.

94

A few days later (when I still haven't been arrested for what I did to Avery Taylor and nobody has told Harry), Philippe and Cynthia invite me on the raft.

"Did you tell?" I snap.

"Tell what?" Cynthia's eyes are very big.

God's bones. "Did you tell about the dumpster? Did you tell your mother or anyone else what we were doing?"

She backs up as my eyes ignite.

"I didn't tell anybody. Why would I do that? Philippe told me why you did it and I think it was very brave. I want to be your friend, not tell on you all the time. We just wanted you to come out on the raft. You can bring your dog."

I glare at Philippe.

"She didn't tell, all right? She just wants to be friends." He is not wearing his coat.

I snort at them both. "And Augustus can come?"

"He'll make everything more fun," Cynthia says. "If I had a dog, I would want a dog just like Augustus and I would bring him everywhere and he would be my best friend. My mama says I can't have a dog, but if I could, I would bring him on the raft with me. I would want a dog that could swim just in case we fall off. Can your dog swim, Rosie?"

"Of course he can swim, Cynthia. He can do anything he wants." I hold up my hand to stop another elephant stampede from rushing out of her mouth.

Augustus thinks it's the best idea in ten thousand years and I have to stop him from eating all the worms. I bring Harry's fishing pole and the life jackets he bought at Walmart.

After I calm down, I start feeling grateful that they are okay about bringing a dog. Not everyone would be, because the chances of flipping over are pretty high, especially with a big galumph like Augustus. This makes me think a little more about friends and what you have to put up with to have some.

It is good to be on the water. There is the slowly drifting raft, the peaceful feeling in your heart, and Augustus is sitting up, watching me cast the line, thumping his tail.

Harry believes in teaching all kids to fish, and it turns out I am excellent at it. "What about your papa? Can he fish, too?" Cynthia wants to know. "My father left before I was born, but if I had a real papa like you do, I would want one who could fish."

"Mind your business," I tell her.

I settle back, look up at the clouds overhead. I eat a huge chunk of the gooey chocolate chip banana cake that Mrs. Salvatore packed for us ("Good Lord, you better not share it with that dog").

I pull out the black-and-white-speckled notebook that I bring everywhere now. I am finding that if I tell myself I will write just three sentences, before I know it, I have filled a page and my whole life is gushing out. Mr. Peterson was right. Writing does light a fire. "Have you been to see your papa?" Cynthia wants to know. "If I had one in the hospital, I would go visit."

Philippe punches her in the arm. The raft tips. "Will you just shut up, Cynthia?"

"I just wanted to know what it's like. If I had a papa in the hospital, I would want to know what it feels like."

Augustus whines for cake. Cynthia says, "I won't tell."

I give a chunk to Augustus, write some more.

I don't want to tell them, because some things are your own business, but this is what it's like to lose your papa.

You dream about him. And pretty much it's always the same dream. It's like you leave a thread in the morning to pick up the next night, and here's what happens.

I am doing something, like maybe being in Miss Holloway's class, or riding the Blackbird or watching my Gloaty Gus galloping through the sandpits, and then for some reason I remember my papa and why have I forgotten him? He's been waiting for me the whole time.

And in my dream I drop what I am doing. Usually it is homework or something I don't want to do and I throw it on the ground but sometimes it's a piece of cake that doesn't taste so good anymore and I race off to find my papa. I can't breathe from running so hard and my heart is pounding. And I have to run about a thousand miles and I can't go fast enough, *I can't go fast enough*—and I fly through wet sand and rush through ponds and jump over sandpits and sometimes all of a sudden I am on my bike but I don't remember pulling it out of the toolshed or even climbing on.

And then finally, finally, my papa is standing right in front of me. And he is saying, *Where have you been?* and my thoughts are clanging and interrupting each other and then my papa is fading away and I am whispering, *No, no, don't go—I just got here,* and then he is all faded but he can still whisper in my ear.

And he is saying, *I am right here and I will never leave you.*

95

One day when I am finally ready, Augustus and I walk up to St. Camillus. There is English ivy twirling at the gate and some of the roses are still in bloom. I am glad for that.

We sit on the bench and wait for Harry. There are pink geraniums here and somebody planted a row of late-blooming chrysanthemums because school starts next week and fall is nearly here.

My very bad dog Augustus wants to jump up right beside me and of course I have to let him and then he wants the best spot on the bench and that means he pushes his big old lumpy moose self right on top of me.

"Move over, you big lug. I have a story to tell you."

Finally, when he is done thumping his tail and licking the grit off my face, I open the first page in the black-and-white-speckled notebook, where I start with how I, Rosie Gillespie, am unsinkable.

"*When you lose your papa, there's a hole in your heart,*" I read.

My Gloaty Gus sighs. So I keep going.

"*But sometimes, if you're very lucky, you get a dog—a big lumpy pain in the neck who jumps out windows and chases the milk truck.*" Augustus wags his tail and then a cat runs by and I grab his collar just in time because he has that thing about cats. Then I scratch between his ears, which he likes very much. His eyes close.

"Don't fall asleep, you big galumph. I'm reading to you." My dog opens one eye and raises an ear and thumps his tail and my heart swells to the size of Jupiter because I know the true way of things.

I know what it's like to love a dog.

96

Harry is carrying a paper bag of flags when he reaches us.

I push over and give him room. I think about cutting some of the roses and taking them in to see my papa, but I don't because that is Harry's job and he will do it when he goes in after me.

I told my grandpa I want to go in without him so I can tell my papa how I am getting on. I will tell him all about my Gloaty Gus and how I found him and how my papa was right all along about Swanson, about how she never had anything but now maybe she will. I'll tell him I'm not moving to California and how Avery Taylor hasn't bothered Swanson again. So far I haven't been caught.

My grandpa tries to give me a few flags to take in. "If you would just put a little time into this . . ."

I roll my eyes before he finishes. *God's bones.*

I tell my very bad dog Augustus that he better keep four paws on the floor and no jumping up on my papa's bed to steal the fattest pillow. He can sit and sniff, that is all, maybe whine a little to let my papa know he is there, and thump his tail when I am reading and we get to the good parts.

Harry got special permission for me to bring my Gloaty Gus inside. He believes in stretching the truth when you have to. They don't let dogs in St. Camillus unless they are trained therapy dogs, with proper visiting manners, so my grandpa bought a bright orange dog vest at Walmart and told the doctor it just so happens that Augustus is a therapy dog for the sight-impaired. None better.

I hand Harry my notebook. I can't carry everything *and* manage my dog. After I visit my papa, my grandpa is driving me out to Mr. Peterson's because nearly three-quarters of the pages are filled. Harry said enough's enough.

"Don't read it," I tell Harry.

"You think I got time to read your rooster scratch? I'm taking a nap." He leans back and pulls his fishing hat over his eyes.

I stand up, take a step toward my papa, and sit back down again.

Harry clears his throat from under his hat, sounding more goose than grandpa.

My Gloaty Gus watches me with those gooseberry eyes and I know he knows what I am feeling about everything. A year is a long time to lose your papa. I scruff the fur on his neck the way he likes and scratch his back and then I stand up and tuck *The World Book of Unbelievable and Spectacular Things* under my arm and together we walk up the steps of St. Camillus—and toward all the beeping.

97

A few days later, when it's too hot for the fire escape, I bring the lemonade and the box of strawberry Popsicles that Harry bought at Walmart and sit out between the toolshed and the maple tree with Philippe and Cynthia.

I brace myself for Cynthia to rev up her motormouth about Avery Taylor or my mum or my visits to see my papa or even to ask about if I got into Mr. Peterson's class after I showed him the notebook, but for a while, at least, the heat is too much for even her.

I am trying harder with both of them, which isn't an easy thing when you think about it.

Philippe begins counting cans. Five black yard-sized garbage bags sit beside us, stuffed full. He opens the ledger he keeps for his recycling profits. His coat is lying in a heap on the grass.

"How much?" Cynthia says, Popsicle juice already running down her hands.

"At least five dollars per bag."

I am bored to death in thirty seconds. "Swanson's roof is leaking something awful," I cut in. I give Augustus some lemonade. He slurps like a horse.

I turn to Philippe. "Will you help me nail some new boards up there? We can use Harry's tools."

"She shoots squirrels, Rosie," Cynthia blurts out. Her hair is brushed, and I don't see the nest underneath. I wonder how that happened.

Philippe writes in his ledger. "I already told you I'm never going back there again."

"Please," I say, sitting up on my heels, trying to find a cool spot in the shade. "My papa told me she doesn't have anything and never did. But now she could have us."

Without looking up from the ledger, Philippe says, "I'm too busy. And it's hot."

"But we can't just let it leak like that. And she's got a really nice dog. And she makes the best sandwiches of my life."

"Forget it, Rosie."

Cynthia stops her Popsicle midair. "But I like to help people, Philippe, I really do, I did ever since I was little, and maybe it's just like Rosie always says, maybe Swanson doesn't shoot squirrels or chase kids or all the other awful things folks say she does. I've never actually seen her do it, have you? Maybe it's just people being mean. Did you ever think about that part, that maybe some people are just dumb and wrong, the same way they sometimes are about us?" She takes a teeny breath. "So maybe we should help her. What kind of sandwiches are they, anyway, Rosie?"

Philippe scoffs and turns back to his cans.

"I'll tell you what," I say, kicking off my flip-flops and pushing my toes into the grass. "I'll help you load all the cans in the back of my grandpa's truck. I bet he'll take you to the recycling center. It's too hot to walk. And I'll come, too, and I'll help and then maybe I'll go out canning with you sometimes—I mean, I'll see if I like it."

I slow myself down because, *God's bones*, I sound like Cynthia.

But I'm not nearly done. "All I really need, Philippe, is for you to help me get up on the roof. I just need a boost. And friends do things for each other."

My eyes want to glare at him, but they don't.

"That's a two-way street, Rosie." He wipes the wet curls off his neck, reaches for another Popsicle. "It's not one-way, with everybody doing stuff for you all the time."

"Yes," says Cynthia. "I can't believe you don't know that yet, Rosie."

"I know that, *Cynthia*," I snap, pulling Augustus over and scratching all up and down his back the way he likes until he gets that grin on his face. "Doesn't it sound like I already know that? Now, do you both want to help me or not?"

98

Harry says I snore like a donkey.

He says only Augustus snores louder than me.

Hornets whirl when my grandpa talks like this, I can tell you that. I toss the spatula I am using to flip our eggs and it lands on the floor.

Louse-head.

Harry's brows march right across the table. "You both in that little room, sawing like old men, shaking the whole building—you're worse than the train, for Pete's sake. From now on, you're sleeping in the shed."

Augustus looks up from his spot under the kitchen table, wondering if you can make kids and their dogs sleep in toolsheds. I know that you can't.

That's when I see the crinkling around Harry's eyes and a smile just starting. I snort and turn up the flame and let the eggs sizzle until they are hard in the middle, not gooey and running all over town the way Harry likes.

I wait for him to yell at me about when am I going to learn to fry a proper egg. But he doesn't. Instead, he comes over and puts an arm around me.

Harry's shirt scratches and his whiskers hurt. His hug isn't the same as my papa's (who knows all about children and their feelings), but it's solid as cement.

My Gloaty Gus raises one ear and thumps his tail. There's an upward curve on my grandpa's face that points toward something hopeful, something new. Augustus and I can't help but notice.

The train roars into town, clanging along the tracks, rattling our walls, sifting grit through the window screens.

I let the spatula stay on the floor and the eggs sizzle.

Harry's hug smells just like Listerine.

ACKNOWLEDGMENTS

I am sincerely grateful to my inspiring editor, Michelle Frey, and her team at Knopf Books for Young Readers: Kelly Delaney, Stephen Brown, and Marisa DiNovis; my encouraging agent, Elizabeth Harding; my writing friend (and former fifth-grade teacher) Laurie Smith Murphy; my parents; my husband, Steven, who reads all my manuscripts over and over again; our four children, Daniel, Matthew, Kate, and Laura; the donut shop in Milford, Massachusetts, where I worked to help put myself through college (and learned so much about life in the process); and the three dogs that we have loved, Norman, Sally, and now Harper—because, as Rosie knows, life is better when you love a dog.